M000035669

SCHOOL OF BROKEN DREAMS

ACADEMY OF SOULS BOOK 3

C.R. JANE
MILA YOUNG

School of Broken Dreams by C. R. Jane and Mila Young

Copyright © 2019 by C. R. Jane and Mila Young

This book is a work of fiction. Names, characters, businesses, places, events, locales, and incidents are either the products of the author's imagination or used in a fictitious manner. Any resemblance to actual persons, living or dead, or actual events is purely coincidental.

To anyone who's found themselves at a fork in the road and taken the one that has monsters.

JOIN C.R. JANE'S READERS' GROUP

Stay up to date with C.R. Jane by joining her Facebook readers' group, C.R.'s Fated Realm. Ask questions, get first looks at new books/series, and have fun with other book lovers!

Join C.R's Fated Realm

JOIN MILA YOUNG'S READERS' GROUP

Join Mila Young's Wicked Readers Group to chat directly with Mila and other readers about her books, enter giveaways, and generally just have loads of fun!

Join Mila Young's Wicked Readers

JOIN C.R./MILA'S JOINT READERS' GROUP

Join C.R./Mila's Joint Readers' Group to chat directly with C.R. & Mila and other readers about their cowrites, enter giveaways, and generally just have loads of fun!

Join Fallen World Series Group

SCHOOL OF BROKEN DREAMS

Raven Academy has dark secrets and Adeline Jones is going to discover them all.

Since starting at Raven Academy, I've seen my fair share of strangeness, things I can't explain, things that shouldn't exist, but this...this is a new level of terrifying.

I no longer know who I am, but one thing's for sure. I love them.

But my love might get us all killed.

"I talk of dreams,
Which are the children of an idle brain,
Begot of nothing but vain fantasy."

— ROMEO AND JULIET- WILLIAM SHAKESPEARE

PROLOGUE

Since starting at Raven Academy, I've seen my fair share of strangeness, things I can't explain, things that shouldn't exist, but this…this is a new level of terrifying.

Dixon is straddling Mercy's body as she lies in bed and he seems to be drinking from her. It is the only way to describe what he's doing. A wave of white mist rises from Mercy's gaped mouth and he inhales it into his mouth. His eyes are completely rolled back into his head and I only see the whites like whatever he's doing is giving him more pleasure than he can take. He's making a disgusting slurping sound that sickens me, makes me want to hurl.

He was her guardian at this school… we've all been appointed protectors since the killings. Except it turns out he might be the murderer who our protectors were supposed to be guarding us against to begin with…he might be the psychopath on our campus. And I've just caught him.

I can't move, I can't make sense of anything. All I can do is stare into those vicious red eyes that promise me pain and retribution for catching and discovering his secret. His upper lip curls inward, revealing sharpened canines.

Incomprehensive cries fall from my lips.

The room tilts around me as it's all so complicated. The mysteries, the deaths. The way the school brushed over the last two deaths. Did the teachers know about Dixon?

A shadow lingers behind him… someone else is in the room with Dixon and Mercy. I can't breathe.

My heart won't stop racing…it's trying to burst through my ribcage and escape.

I should be running for help, but I can't unstick my feet.

Dixon gets an eager sadistic gleam in his eye as he seems to come to a decision.

Then the other person in the room peers around the corner at me, and I see him. My mouth drops open.

Mercy's ex… the neighbor she had a crush on, the guy who did drugs…the one I thought had killed Bethanie. What is he doing in the room with Dixon?

Mercy's ex suddenly spins on his heels and catapults himself through the window in Mercy's room, glass shattering like my broken sanity, tossed into thousands of shards of a puzzle I just can't put together.

Dixon faces me and he lunges for me, eyes huge, mouth gaping.

My scream lashes out as fear strangles me, and my knees buckle under me.

CHAPTER 1

(ALEXANDER)

I'm tempted to try to find a necromancer to bring this fuckwad back to life, just so I can have the pleasure of killing him. His head was lying next to him when we found him, brutally hacked off like whoever had done it had been in a rage when it happened. The guy had more restraint than I would have had if I had discovered him first though. He would be in pieces if I had seen him attacking Adeline.

If she dies because of him...I will figure out a way to punish him in the next life.

I crouch down next to Dixon's body, my hands trembling with rage as I look at the wound, trying to get a clue who in the school would have enough strength to put down an almost fully grown one of our kind.

"You should go see her," says Finn, laying a hand on my shoulder. I'm so wrapped up in my own misery and anger, that I didn't even hear him approach.

"How is she doing?" I ask him in a choked-up voice.

"Still here," he says, and I can tell that he's trying not to cry as well. We've fallen for her. Now a life without her seems impossible, and I'm not sure how we will all survive if she's no longer in our lives. I can only pray that our suspicions about what she is are true.

"And her friend?" I ask, feeling irrational anger at Mercy for putting Adeline in danger even though I know Mercy was just as much a victim as Adeline was in all of this.

"She's packing up to go home. I haven't been able to get a real word out of her. She just cries. I can feel the guilt seeping out of her. It was almost impossible not to feed, it was so strong."

I look at him sharply, and he gives me an annoyed stare. "I said 'almost.' I didn't feed on her," he responds stiffly. I nod and look back at the corpse in front of us.

"Who do you think did this?" Finn asks.

I'm just about to answer him, when a voice that I've grown to hate, chimes in. "I did," announces Connor Whitehouse.

Finn and I spin around to look at him incredulously. Connor is indeed standing there, a cocky smirk on his face as he glances at the body. Dixon's fangs are still extended, and Connor looks non-plussed at the sight. But how would a human have been able to take down Dixon...unless...

I stand up with a growl, my fangs threatening to extend. I take a deep breath to see if I can smell anything special about him.

Nothing.

That's odd.

I can't smell anything. Not a human smell, not a supernatural smell. Nothing.

The monster inside of me begins to swell as it realizes that Connor might be a wolf in sheep's clothing that's been walking around my school. Around my girlfriend.

I step towards him.

"What are you?" I hiss, still sniffing the air as I try to get a clue about what he is. I've never encountered a being who had carried no scent before.

Connor grins at me, fangless teeth shining brightly. "Trying to figure me out?" he taunts me. I take another step towards him, and I can feel the monster emerging in Finn next to me. "Do you want to waste time fighting a losing battle with me, or do you want to catch the other vampire who was in the room?" asks Connor snidely.

His question stops me in my tracks. I look at Finn who looks as confused as I am. I look back at Connor. "What are you talking about? There was someone else in the room with Dixon and Mercy?" I don't bother asking him how he knows about vampires. I can push him on that later. Right now, I need to concentrate on the other threat facing Adeline.

"Care to go hunting?" he asks. It might be a trap, but I'm concerned enough about the possibility of someone else being out there who wants to attack Adeline that I decide to go along with him. And despite his bravado, it's very unlikely that he's even close to as good of a fighter as I am. I'm sure I can handle anything he throws at me.

"Lead the way," I tell him. I glance at Finn. "Go stay with Adeline," I order. He seems torn, and I know that he's itching to go after the other rogue responsible for hurting Adeline.

"Nyx and Dante are with her," he argues.

"We need to make sure they don't do anything rash with their emotions so heightened," I remind him. Dante and Nyx have always been the less disciplined of the four of us. I need to make sure that they don't do anything if Adeline gets worse and needs more help.

My reminder is enough to get him to listen to me and I watch as he heads towards Adeline's room.

Connor and I walk through the halls. We stop in front of one of the stone walls and I glance at him confused. He presses on one of the stones right above his head, and a dark passageway suddenly appears as a section of the wall fades away. I look at him in astonishment. I thought I knew every secret that the school possessed. How has he only been here for a few weeks and managed to find something I didn't know about?

"Let's go," he says as he crouches down to go through the entryway. It's pitch black in there and I hesitate for a moment about being at a disadvantage if Connor does decide to attack me. Connor sticks his head out. "Are you coming or not? I don't want him to get too far. I'm not going to kill you in here... At least not tonight," he says with a smirk.

I snarl at him but follow him into the dark abyss. The wall closes behind me and there's nothing but blackness around me... and silence. Connor suddenly moves, and I crouch down into a defensive position preparing for an attack. But instead of attacking me, he turns on his phone's flashlight. I feel like an idiot, and I want to punch him for the smug look on his face.

Connor wisely chooses not to say anything about my reaction and instead begins to set off down the narrow corridor. It's musty and damp and the number of cobwebs I'm seeing tells me it's been a while since someone's walked through here. We walk for about five minutes before we stop in front of another wall. Connor starts pressing on the stones in front of him, and after a few tries a section of the wall once again disappears and I can smell the sharp scent of the nighttime air and feel the cold breeze as it blows through the space in the wall.

Sure enough, we were outside in half the time that it would've taken going another way. Connor steps outside first, his eyes darting around. He freezes and sniffs the air. I'm off my game right now. Between the attack on Adeline, discovering that Dixon is one of the culprits attacking students, and the appearance of Connor, it's hard to keep my mind on the task at hand. I shake my head, trying to get my mind straight. Following his lead, I sniff the air and immediately find the decaying scent of a vampire who has recently fed. Whoever it is hasn't taken blood tonight, he's taken something much stronger and more filling... a soul.

We start off on a brisk jog, following the scent. It gets stronger as we head into the forest. He must have fed a lot, because not even all the smells of the forest with its creatures and everything else can mask him. He's traveling fast, not doing anything to hide his path. There are trampled leaves and tree branches that mark the way behind him. He's in a hurry and he's amped up from feeding on Mercy's soul and whoever else he has gorged himself on over the last few weeks.

Eager to get this over with, I put on a burst of speed that not even

Connor can match. It takes another half an hour, but I finally catch up to our target when he stops to take a break, I'm sure thinking that the threat of anyone following him is over with.

I've never seen this guy before. He's wearing a leather vest like he's some kind of wannabe biker. He has tattooed sleeves on both arms, his head is shaved, and he's got piercing in both ears. Not a guy that I would've missed walking around the school. He's definitely who we've been looking for. I can smell Mercy's soul wafting from him. She has an unusual taste to her, one that makes her a target for regular feedings from some of the other students. Probably too many feedings if I'm being honest. It probably explains her kooky nature.

Connor appears a second later beside me and I can't hold back my grin at the fact that he just ate my dust. He lets out a small grunt as he rolls his eyes. We turn our focus from our dick measuring contest back to the matter at hand. It's only a matter of time though before this fragile truce between the two of us goes up in flames.

It takes a moment, but I see when Mr. Tattoos catches our scent and realizes that he is still being hunted.

For a moment he contemplates running, and then acceptance flashes across his face.

"Come out, come out, wherever you are," he yells out tauntingly, even though I can smell the fear that's starting to seep from his pores.

Grinning widely, I step into the grove where he's been resting. A look of alarm flashes on his face before he quickly schools it into one of nonchalance.

"Well, if it isn't Alexander Dachnavar. I wouldn't have expected to see you here of all people. Unless you have discovered the little secret that Adeline Jones is hiding as well."

I keep my face blank, knowing that there's no way that he can leave here alive. He's not just dangerous because he's been attacking students and could attack Adeline. He's dangerous because he somehow knows what she is.

"And what secret is that?" I ask him dismissively, like I'm confident that he doesn't have anything that would interest me. My attitude does the trick in poking his pride. By the looks of him, we've never run in the same circles. And he seems to know exactly who I am, meaning he knows the power that I hold in the community, and the fact that my mother is on the Council. Power that he has never experienced.

"Can't help but hear the rumblings that the angels have made a reappearance. Or correction that one angel has made an appearance. I bet her soul tastes like ambrosia, it will be the best thing I'll ever taste once I get my hands on her," he rambles. "I'm sure you've experienced it already. Mercy's told me all about the little harem that Miss Jones has been collecting of you and your friends. There's no way you've been able to stop yourself from tasting that."

My hands clench. It's a small movement, but he notices it and it tells him exactly what he wants to know. That he's right.

I'll be having some words with Adeline after this...if she wakes up, that she needs to keep better friends.

Adeline Jones is special, and her secret is one worth fighting for.

"What's your game plan here?" I ask him with a smirk. I can see the anticipation building in his eyes as he thinks about what awaits him if he makes it out of here alive.

He laughs at my question. "She changes everything, Alexander. You know that, right?"

I try to smile back, but I'm sure it looks a little crazy by the fact that he takes a step backwards. He stops himself and crouches down, growling low and menacingly at me. I'm sure it would make a human pee himself, but it's nothing to me. I'm a far scarier predator than anything he could offer.

Connor steps into the grove next to me, his face a picture of boredom. "Are you going to continue to play with your food?" he asks me. I want to punch him in the face, but I refrain.

"I'm going to have her," the vamp hisses, and there's a hint of desperation threaded throughout his voice, like it's a need rather than a want.

"You'll have to get in line then," responds Connor.

Growling again, our prey crouches even lower to the ground, preparing to spring at me at a moment's notice. Before he can take a breath, I move. Hitting him so hard that it knocks him back at least 30 feet into a large tree that topples from the impact. The sound of him impacting the tree makes a large cracking noise that echoes through the woods. If it was any other creature that I had punched, they would be dead. But unfortunately, vamps are a little stronger than that and it's wishful thinking that this could be over already.

It takes a minute, he pulls himself from the wreckage of the tree, picking off pieces of bark that have attached themselves to his vest. Smiling at Connor and I, he rips a large branch off the fallen tree and flings it at me. It embeds itself in the tree directly behind where I'd been standing a millisecond ago.

Before I can react, Connor has pounced on the guy who is still 30 feet away. The two become locked in a deadly struggle, each one trying to tear the other apart. Gripping a large branch off another tree, I fling it at the two of them, not particularly caring which one it hits. Connor flings himself out of the way just in time, glaring at me incredulously as he does so. I casually shrug my shoulders as if I hadn't just almost impaled him.

Our tattooed friend recovers faster than Connor. Picking up a large rock in the clearing, he draws his arm back and throws it at me faster than a human would be able to track it. It hits me in the shoulder before I can get away and knocks me backwards, ricocheting into another tree.

The fact that I let this poser hit me with anything just shows how off my game I am at the moment, and I decide enough is enough. I pick up another large branch and run at him, holding it like I would a javelin. He tries to run, but there's no stopping me. I throw the branch, crushing his skull, and he collapses in a heap to the ground. Taking another branch, I impale it into his heart, making sure that he won't be bothering anyone at the school again, let alone telling anyone Adeline's secrets.

I look over at Connor, who is trying to not look impressed by my kill.

"You obviously have some explaining to do," I tell him staunchly.

"But I need to get back to Adeline. Make no mistake though, you will be giving me answers. I'm not someone that you can mess with."

A muscle in Conner's cheek twitches. "I look forward to our talk," he responds.

I pull a flask out of my pocket before throwing some branches on top of the vampire's corpse. Flicking the top off I pour the contents all over his body. Students who've seen it think that I carry it around in case I need a drink, but you never know when you're going to need to burn a body. Pulling a lighter out of my other pocket, I set him on fire.

I walk away without another glance at Connor. My fight with him will be another day.

Right now, I just need to get to my girl. A girl that I don't know I can live without.

CHAPTER 2

(ADELINE)

"*A*deline," a familiar male's voice calls to me.

I stir from sleep; my eyes crack open to bright light and I wince as they adjust to the brightness floating in from the window. Exhaustion wracks through me. I don't remember ever feeling so lethargic.

Slowly, my vision comes into focus as does Connor Whitehouse's face. The guy I had a crush on for so long at my old school, the guy who gave me my first heartbreak. He had shown up at Raven Academy unexpectedly. And there's something just not right about him. Something I can't put my finger on.

"How are you feeling?" he asks, sitting on the bed next to me with a concerned look on his face.

I shuffle upright in my bed, and panic strangles me as I find myself in my dorm room. "How did you get in here...how did I get in here?"

My brain is still playing catch-up from the cobwebs. Suddenly an image of red eyes fills my mind. I remember... I had passed out after finding Mercy with Dixon and her ex. Dixon came for me...and my memory goes fuzzy after that.

My stomach churns with sickness though and I realize again how weak I'm feeling. Like I could sleep for days.

My veins freeze as the image of Mercy passed out on her bed appears in my thoughts.

"Mercy," I cry, and I try to shove the blankets off of me. "I have to see her."

"She's okay," Connor assures me, not bothering to move from the side of the bed and get out of my way.

"She can't be. She was attacked. I saw her." I feel the blood drain from my face as I remember the image of Dixon on top of her. "Get out of my way, Connor," I snap.

"Adeline, you need to stay in bed until you feel better."

Fury bubbles in my chest. "I'm just a little tired, and why are you in my room, again?"

"There's a roster for your lovers to watch over you, and I volunteered. You fainted, remember?"

I go rigid at his words and scratch the back of my neck, trying to sort my jumbled memories and thoughts. "So Mercy's okay?" I ask suspiciously, not sure if I believe him.

"You need to just rest a bit, okay?" But he isn't exactly answering my question either.

"We have to talk," he begins as he turns his head to glance at the closed door of my room and then back at me.

"I have nothing to say to you." In truth I had many words to say to him about everything he had put me through, but I barely had enough energy to string a sentence together at the moment.

He twists around to face me. "Do you even know what's going on at this school, Adi?"

"Yeah, someone's killing the students. Dixon and Mercy's ex apparently."

"I've known you for a long time, Adi. Are you really this... obtuse?"

I bristle. "I resent that. Get the hell out of my room now before I scream." Who in the world did he think he was?

"Okay, I admit that was a low blow, but you have to listen to me." He grabs my arm, his fingers strong as iron. "Your life's in danger, and I can protect you."

I break out laughing and shuffle out of bed on the opposite side in slow sluggish movements, pulling free from him, noting I am still wearing my uniform. Why was I so tired?

Just then the door to my room bursts open and Braxton sweeps into the room. Looking worried, but as strong and handsome as ever. Those deep emerald eyes find me in an instant, concern burrowing behind them. "Adeline, are you okay?"

"Perfect. Connor was just leaving." I wrap my arms around my middle, standing across the bed from them both, feeling awkward at their presence in my room.

Connor climbs off the bed and just stares at me with intensity, like he's trying to make me read his thoughts. Why is he acting so weird?

He mouths the words, 'Don't trust them' just as he'd told me back at camp.

And especially don't trust the teachers, he'd said on the trip.

"We'll talk later," he murmurs in my direction and turns to leave the room.

Once he's gone, Braxton shuts the door and closes the distance between us in three long strides. "Did he hurt you?"

I shake my head. Despite how much Connor annoys me, I just want him out of my way, not for the other guys in my life to start paying him the wrong attention.

"What happened to Mercy and Dixon? How did I get here?"

Braxton reaches for me, his hand gently cupping the side of my face, eyeing me up and down as if searching for evidence of bruises.

Being so close to him always affects me, leaving me daydreaming of kissing him, my mind emptying of every other problem. Except, this time my heart is banging too loud and panic is slithering down my spine.

Something isn't right and I have to know what is going on.

"I need to see, Mercy," I explain, my insides tight as a knot, unable to get the image of her unconscious on the bed out of my head.

Braxton's brow furrows. "I have something to share with you," he says, like he's about to deliver the worst news ever. The uncertainty in his eyes remind me of the same look Mom gave me when she explained Dad had cancer. When she broke the news, my world shattered. And now I stand here, trembling, staring at Braxton, too scared to voice a word.

"With your recent blood test and Dixon's attack, I--"

I stare down at myself, studying my arms, feeling my body for any hints of the attack. I vividly recall him lunging for me with those violent eyes.

"What are you doing?" Braxton asks.

"Dixon lunged for me when I passed out, but you say he attacked me like someone witnessed it after I fainted. Wouldn't I have some bruises or wounds on my body as evidence?"

"That's the thing I'm trying to tell you. You survived because you're not exactly human. You have angel blood in your veins." He speaks so casually that I wait for him to burst out laughing and tell me this is some ridiculous joke. But he doesn't.

I blink through my confusion, staring at Braxton like he's grown horns. "Angel blood?" I squeak.

His hand is on mine, so tender that it coaxes me to believe anything he says. Except the words coming from his mouth make no sense.

Angel blood. What did that mean? Is that a euphemism for calling me an angel?

He clears his throat. "Angels exist, Adeline. As does Heaven. I got ahold of the blood samples and they showed there was something abnormal about your blood...the angelic compound ey' was present in large amounts. And after you survived Dixon's attack, well, now it's clear what you are."

I blow out a frustrated breath and shift on the bed. "None of what you just said makes sense." But the blood tests stick in my mind... they said I am an O negative. My parents are B and AB positive, so they apparently aren't my real parents. But that doesn't mean I have angel blood. Do angels even have blood types? What is an ey' compound?

Why am I even considering it as an option? There's no way that angels exist.

"I don't know why you're saying this to me," I murmur. "It's not funny, and I'm not feeling the greatest at the moment."

"Adeline, you need to rest. You will soon start to realize what I'm saying is true. And I'll be here for you, to help you."

"Help me how?" The room is tilting around me. "Are you an angel too?" I half laugh, half cringe at how insane I sound.

He wraps his strong arms around me, and I let myself soften against his hard chest, hating how lost and confused I feel. How his words leave me floating in a bubble.

"You need to rest now, and we'll talk more when you wake up."

I break free and offer him a clumsy, demure smile. "You're probably right." I push myself under the blankets as he reaches over and slides a loose lock behind an ear.

"I'll be right outside," he tells me, and I don't think to question him about that.

When he leaves my room, I flop back down, roll onto my back, and try to make sense of what he just said.

Have I entered the Twilight Zone or am I still dreaming? I can't think of any other explanation. Braxton has always been a man who speaks straight forward. And he's never been one to make jokes, but to say I had angel blood in me couldn't be anything else but me hallucinating.

The next couple of hours fly past in a mindless blur and confusion as I try to get more sleep. I finally end up falling in and out of dreams that have me flying through the air.

When the floorboard in my room creaks, my eyes flip open to Braxton walking into my room. I soften back in bed, and shuffle upright to sit in bed.

"Did I imagine all of that?" I ask him hesitantly.

He looks at me sympathetically. "Believe me, I wish you had. But it's all true, Adeline. If you think back, have strange things ever happened to you?"

"Like what?" I ask, not able to think of anything particularly unique about my life thus far.

"When was the last time you were sick?" he asks, sitting next to me on the bed.

I open my mouth to respond but realize that I can't. I can't think of the last time that I was sick. Or anytime that I was sick. "When you scrape yourself, are you fine a few hours later? Do bruises disappear quickly as well? Do people seem to have strong reactions to you," he continues.

As I think about everything that he's saying, I begin to panic. This doesn't mean that I'm some sort of mythological creature, but there are some strange things about myself that I don't really have any explanation for. And there's that fact again that my parents aren't really my real parents...

"I'm sure there's an explanation for all of that," I murmur as my mind races.

"I just gave you the explanation, Adeline," he says gently.

Suddenly I become very aware of how close he's sitting to me, how good he smells, how much I want him every time I see him.

There's a strange look in his eyes, as if I'm the very air that he needs to breathe. My thoughts settle as we continue to stare at each other. My attention all of a sudden becomes laser focused on his perfect face. I've never felt so wanted like I do at this moment. He's looking at me like I'm his everything.

* * *

(Braxton)

"What is it?" she whispers self-consciously.

"I almost lost you," I whisper as my eyes devour the healthy glow that has finally returned to her cheeks. The image of her white and lifeless on the ground haunts my dreams.

I don't wait a second more before I pull her into my chest. Everything feels right again when she holds me back. Her cheek rests against my shoulder as I whisper to her, "I've made so many mistakes, but pushing you away is my greatest sin." I kiss her hair, her forehead, every inch of her that I can without letting her go.

"I love you, Adeline, I think I have since the moment I saw you. And I'll tell you every day." I run my hand over the back of my neck and throw my head back to mutter, "Twenty fucking times a day," before looking back into her beautiful blue eyes. "Whatever it takes for you to believe it."

She stares back at me without saying a word, just watching me spill every bit of truth to her that I have. I whisper my greatest insecurity, "I can't lose you. I won't survive it."

Adeline's hesitation kills me, every second making me exceedingly more nervous that this is the end. "I don't think I'm cut out for this world," she tells me. "Angels and demons. They were myths, mythical creatures that I read about in books. And now you're trying to tell me that they're real. And that I'm one of them."

"I wish I could take this from you," I tell her, thinking of the secrets that I'm still keeping from her.

"If angels and demons are real, which one are you?" she whispers to me, and I want to tell her the truth just then. But angels don't belong in hell, and I've been living there since I was born. I'll lose her when she knows, and I don't want to have to live without feeling her love for at least one night.

I kiss her instead of answering, and when I pull back, I can see the hope in her eyes that this time I won't run from her. That this time it will be real.

Little does she know that she's the realest thing I've ever had in my life.

"You really love me?" Adi asks me and I hate that she questions it. "Of course I do. I mean it when I say I always have," I tell her, pushing the hair from her face. "I love you, Adeline. I'll spend every day proving it to you if I have to."

I just hope that I'll get the chance.

The tips of her fingers glide down my forearm as she looks me in the eyes and says, "I love you, too."

I already knew she did. What I don't know though, is if it's enough. If I'm enough as I am to keep her.

"I just want you." Her words come out raw and full of nothing but the truth.

"Don't leave me," I beg her, even though she won't understand what I'm asking of her. She closes her eyes and rests her head on my shoulder. "I promise I won't if you won't," she whispers.

"Then you're mine forever."

"I want you to make me yours," she tells me softly, as she stares up at me.

I'm far from a saint, but the trembling of my body makes me feel like this is my first time. Probably because it's the only time that counts. I've never made love before. It's always been just a release for me. This is something so beyond just a bodily function. This is everything.

I kiss her again like I have a right to, like I've been wanting to every day since the first time she stepped out of that car and changed my life forever. Our stolen moments have only stoked the fire inside of me.

Her lips are soft, and she parts them with a sigh. I take this opportunity to nibble on her bottom lip before slowly kissing her jaw. I try to back away, to stop this before I go too far. She's in a vulnerable place and I can't do this unless I know it's what she really wants. She says she loves me, but I have a suspicion she loves them too, even with all the things they've done to her.

I'll just have to get her to love me so much that there isn't room for them in her heart.

* * *

(Adeline)

He pulls away from me, staring at me like he can see inside of me. And maybe he can. Braxton might not want to tell me what he is, and that may scare me, but I'm in this too deep to be scared away from the unknown.

"Come here," I whisper more huskily than I intended, pulling on his shirt to bring him back down to me.

Complying immediately, Braxton's mouth is back on mine. I welcome him eagerly, returning the passionate thrust and parry of his tongue and arching up to his body. We drink and nip at each other hungrily, hands roaming and bodies straining. Breathing hard, Braxton pushes away from me long enough to pull me up to my knees and grasp the bottom of the loose t-shirt dress I had put on after I'd woken up and got cleaned and dressed early this morning.

I lift my arms to assist him, thankful that I put on a matching bra and panties set.

"You're killing me," Braxton says when he sees what's under my dress. His voice sounds strained, like he's holding himself back. He's stock still, watching me from beneath his dark lashes. His jaw is clenched hard.

I hesitantly put my hands on his t-shirt. He's dressed casually for once, and although I love him in his suit that he wears while teaching, I can't get enough of him like this, jeans and a white t-shirt...hair a mess. It's my kryptonite.

He helps me take his shirt off, and I touch the planes of his chest for the first time, sliding my palms down the perfect muscles that he hides behind his clothes. My heart is beating so hard it feels like it's going to burst out of my chest. I continue my exploration down his body, and when I get to his jeans, he doesn't stop me.

My fingers are shaking as I work to unbutton Braxton's jeans. The bulge under my hand is making them a little hard to manage and every time my fingers brush against him, I hear his breathing change. I didn't know his reaction to my hands on him could cause such a corresponding reaction in me. My body is throbbing and I'm desperate to have him naked.

He's letting me take the lead, but I'm so nervous that I hope he takes over soon before I chicken out. Still shaking, I finally release the last button revealing his tight briefs. Instinctively, I slide my hand inside and curl it around his length. Braxton hisses out a shuddery breath and grabs my wrist.

"I want to touch you." I pout with a small smile over my nerves.

"You will. You can. Whenever you want after this. But I promise you I don't need any help right now. I'm so fucking turned on; I can hardly see straight."

His words set me on fire.

It's hard to understand, in this moment, that I can hold so much power. I hurriedly push his jeans down his thighs, and before he can move to assist me, I shove his briefs down, too. There's something written in Latin in dark swirling script across his left hip bone, but I don't stop to pay attention to it. I'm more interested in what else I'm seeing.

Braxton immediately pushes me back on the bed and kisses me hungrily. I gasp into his mouth at the amazing feel of his skin against mine, his weight settling on me and between my legs. He pushes down my bra and his tongue finds my breast. Within moments I'm literally writhing under him. I arch up, whimpering more as the movement causes his erection to press against my damp underwear. He rocks against me slowly and it feels so good that I'm worried I may be dreaming.

Then he begins to make his way south, kissing down my stomach, stopping to dip his tongue into my belly button. My nerves ratchet up. Dead focused, Braxton slowly peels my panties down my legs. The look on his face sends my pulse into overdrive. I'm panting and completely not in control of my body's reactions. I still as he unhooks the last foot from my underwear and slowly runs his hands up my legs, parting them firmly as he goes, his eyes, and then his mouth following the movement. His touch is a trail of fire up the inside of my thigh. Shifting, Braxton settles himself more firmly between my legs. And now my nerves are through the roof.

"You're the most beautiful thing I've ever seen," Braxton groans, and in this moment, I believe him. Before I can have second thoughts, his mouth is on me, a place where no one else has been like this. I cry out, thrashing against the sensation because it feels better than anything I've ever experienced. He grips my thighs more firmly to keep me in place as his tongue flicks over me.

I let out a moan and it comes out much more high-pitched than I intended.

I squeeze my eyes shut as if that will help me to contain my reaction. It just serves to focus all my senses on the magic he's performing on my body right now.

I'm practically paralyzed with pleasure and sensation, my body tight and prickly as if my skin can't hold the feelings inside me. His mouth is hot and wet, and his tongue seems to know just what to do to my body. His hands join his mouth, and he eases a finger inside me. I grab fistfuls of the sheets. I want him to stop but I also don't. I want to watch him, but I can't.

I'm heading to a precipice that I have little experience with and all I can hope is that he will be there to catch me when I fall. I'm completely lost to sensation as he loves me with his tongue and his fingers. He seems to touch some deep and magical place inside me, because suddenly I'm there, and I'm crying out as I fall apart, arching my hips up into his mouth.

"Fuck," Braxton moans, his voice rough and gravely, his breath labored, matching mine. He places a lingering kiss on my thigh before he makes his way up my body until he's holding himself above me, his green eyes cutting me open. For a moment, four other faces flash in front of me, but I push thoughts of them away. Braxton deserves this to be just us.

The sight of Braxton above me, his eyes staring at me with so much love that it's impossible to doubt him, is almost too much for me to handle. I try to swallow over the lump in my throat as I reach up and run a hand across his beautiful cheekbones. He lets out a long breath. "Where did you go just then?" he asks hesitantly, as if he knows already.

"Nowhere. I don't want to be anywhere else but here," I tell him. And it's the truth. He swallows hard at my words as if he's trying to tamper down his emotions. He holds my gaze as his body rocks forward and I feel him sliding against my wetness.

"I'm scared I'll hurt you," he says gruffly.

I open my legs wider and wrap them around him. "For the first time in my life it will be pain that I want. I need you inside of me. I want you now," I assure him in a choked voice. He told me he wasn't an angel, but I don't believe him in this moment. Hovering above me with a piece of his dark hair falling across his face, his piercing eyes watching me as if I'm everything, he looks like a fallen angel and I want him to drag me down with him wherever he goes.

He lowers his mouth to mine and at the same time he rocks back and then forward as he eases himself into me, stretching me, filling me, completing me. I forget to breathe; I forget who I am. It feels amazing, like I'm where I belong, and I want more.

He's trying to go slow, but I'm so desperate for him, I don't care if it hurts. I rock up against him. He gives in, groaning and plunging his tongue into my mouth in a searing kiss that reaches into my soul. At the same time his hips move forward, taking me completely.

A sharp pain wrenches my mouth from his. For a moment I lose my breath, but I don't let him pull away from me. I don't want him to stop.

"Baby...," he says.

I open my eyes and see him with an anguished look on his beautiful face.

I can't speak at the moment. Not because it still hurts, but because it's too much. Too much of him, too much emotion, too much...of everything.

I squeeze my eyes shut to stop the emotion I know is about to spill out. A drop of moisture leaks out the side of my lashes despite my attempts. I turn my head. I need to say something quickly before he thinks I don't want this. Instead of talking, I turn back and grasp his neck pulling him back down to me and kissing him deeply.

Braxton kisses me back and I slowly move my hips against his until he finally responds. He pulls his mouth away from me and his tongue licks the place my tear had escaped. "Open your eyes, baby" he whispers. After a second, when I've gotten a bit more control over myself, I do, meeting his deep and searching gaze.

"You okay?" His breathing is fast, and I can feel the tension in his body as he tries to hold himself still.

"Yes," I assure him. "It feels ..." I'm not sure how to put into words what he's doing to me.

"Perfect," he finishes for me with a sexy grin, finally starting to move, hard this time. I gasp at his movements and nod. He holds my gaze, moving in and out as I stare back at him. I know I'm looking at him like he's the eighth wonder of the world, but I can see the same feeling reflected back at me in his eyes.

I match his strokes as pleasure starts to build inside of me. I'm aware of all the small changes in his facial expressions as what he is feeling plays across his face like I'm watching a movie. His face is flushed, and his breathing is heavy as he moves. His arms and body quiver with tension and restraint as he braces himself above me.

I see the moment that his restraint snaps, when his movements pick up speed and become slightly erratic.

Watching him lose control is a sight to behold and I try to savor the look on his face, but I can't keep my eyes open as that feeling inside of me continues to build. I gasp under the onslaught, squeezing my eyes shut and writhing up to meet his thrusts.

"Look at me," Braxton rasps out. I snap my eyes open as he plays my body perfectly. He shifts up slightly and I feel as his hand slides between us, touching me perfectly, sending me spiraling into what feels like space as I come hard.

Braxton is no longer holding back as I ride out the waves, gasping and clenching around him as he slams into me several more times before letting go, his face contorted in harsh and beautiful pleasure. "Fuck, Adi."

I draw him down to me, holding his shuddering body tightly as I struggle to get my breath back. I knew the vision of Braxton's face above me as he came undone would be embedded in my mind forever. After a few moments, he relaxes and wraps his arms around me, letting out a deep sigh.

CHAPTER 3

(FINN)

I walk into Alexander's room and I am surprised to see that Braxton, Nyx, and Dante are also there. There's an air of tension in the room, like everyone's about to boil over from the stress of the last few days. Adeline has appeared to be making a full recovery, something I've never been more relieved about.

But it's a double-edged sword. Even when Braxton had confirmed that his tests of her blood showed it possessed the angelic ey' compound only found in heavenly beings, I still had trouble believing it.

Now that she has recovered from a feeding that would have killed any other human being, I can't deny the truth. Adeline has come from an angelic bloodline, and that means that the whole world has suddenly made her their number one target...if they find out.

That's why Alexander had called this meeting tonight. We needed to decide how we were going to somehow protect Adeline. Braxton had already made sure to snag the blood from the school nurse before she could test it properly. Lucky for us, she didn't have the tools necessary to detect the ey' compound, she could only see the trace human blood that Adeline possessed...hence Adeline finding out that her parents weren't her parents, but not anything else about her genetics.

Braxton had switched the vial with another human student's to throw the Council off track. But if things kept happening...like miraculous recoveries, superhuman strength randomly appearing, or god forbid actual wings appearing...

We would be shit out of luck.

"I can smell her all over you," says Alexander suddenly, glaring at Braxton with disdain and seething jealousy. Braxton just smirks at him, quirking his lips but not answering him.

I reach out my senses to see what he's talking about and as soon as I capture the scent that's coating Braxton, I'm hit by a mix of lust and jealousy so strong it knocks me backwards a step. Adeline's arousal is all over Braxton. By the smell of it, somehow Mr. Professor over here made sure that our girl wasn't quite so innocent as she was before. I try to block out the scent since it makes me want to run out of the room, go find Adeline and stake my claim over her. Over and over and over.

The other guys must have just figured it out too because there's yelling and pushing, and even a fist thrown by none other than Nyx. Seeing the chaos clears my head and I give a loud whistle, glad that Alexander has made this room virtually sound proof recently with some kind of device he bought from a regional warlock.

Everyone stops what they're doing and looks at me with surprise. I know why they all look shocked. I'm usually the one who stays behind the scenes, never interfering or taking the lead in anything. I have always been the one to go with the flow. But I can't do that when it comes to Adeline. If these idiots can't see past their own desires to what's best for Adeline themselves...then I'm going to have to make them.

"I think we can all acknowledge that we're all pissed off and jealous about Braxton and Adeline," I begin, instigating a low growl to erupt from Alexander towards Braxton at my understatement at the level of feelings present in the room right now. "But obviously there's nothing we can do about that. Adeline has made it obvious that she has feelings towards all of us, seemingly deep feelings if I'm not just having wishful thinking about how I hope she feels about me." I take a deep breath, looking at each one of them. There's reluctance but burgeoning acceptance as they get what I'm leading up to.

"Adeline's going to need protection. More than just one of us can give to her. I wish I could keep her safe myself, but an angel...fuck. I can't keep her safe from the whole supernatural world myself. I'm not even sure the five of us are enough to keep her safe." I sigh in distress and brush a hand through my hair frustratedly.

"You think we need to all just accept the situation and date her while we're keeping her safe," sums up Nyx.

I nod my head, trying to gauge how they seem to feel about that idea.

There's a long, awkward silence as we all think through our options. It's basically either one of us gets the girl and then loses her because we can't keep her safe. Or we all get the girl and have a chance of keeping her.

If it's a choice between keeping a part of her or losing all of her, I know which option I would pick. I just hope the rest of them are on the same page.

Did I dream of meeting my soul mate and then having to share her? Fuck no. But Adeline has changed a lot of things about the way I think and do things, so it's not a surprise that she would change that as well.

"I'll share her with you assholes if it means that she's safe," Nyx says softly with a swear.

"I will too," says Dante reluctantly, pain written all over his face at the thought.

We all turn our attention to Alexander and Braxton, the two most likely to not want to go along with this plan. They're staring at each other and Alexander has a muscle in his cheek that's twitching. It's like they're playing a game of chicken and trying to see which one of them is going to fold first.

To my surprise, Alexander is.

"I'll do it," he says stiffly. "I'll do anything for her."

There's a promise in his words and it seems to speak to Braxton. He nods his head. "I'm in as well. I don't know how the hell this is going to work, but she's going to need all the help she can get once this news gets out."

We all nod, and I feel a sense of relief at the fact that Adeline is going to have five men invested in keeping her safe no matter what she chooses...or doesn't choose.

"Let's get one thing straight though," says Nyx, capturing our attention. "I don't want to hear any details about what the rest of you jackasses do with Adeline," he continues.

There's a pause and then we all burst out laughing.

This is going to be interesting.

* * *

(Adeline)

The school halls are busy today. Students everywhere, their chatter loud cicadas on hot summer evenings. It reminds me of the hot afternoons I'd sit with Mom and Dad on our back veranda, talking about everything from the myth that a red sky meant rain was coming to how we'd spend a million dollars if we ever won the lottery. Of course, we never spent money on the lottery, but it was fun to dream. They were simple times where I forgot about school, bullying, my crush on Connor, and before my dad fell sick.

I used to think they were complicated days, but nothing could have prepared me for Raven Academy.

My mind leaps back to Braxton in my room, his tenderness, his intoxicating words that will remain with me for an eternity, touches forever imprinted on my mind. No one has ever kissed me the way he has, and he admitted to loving me. My heart hasn't stopped pounding in my chest since he made love to me.

I'm smiling endlessly and can't stop my body from humming. With each move, I feel the slight ache between my thighs that leaves me swooning at what we'd just done.

I always imagined my first time to be clumsy. The magazines said

27

to expect some pain, except Braxton was the opposite. Sweet, affectionate, and treating me as gentle as breakable glass. The heat from our love making sweeps through me and my knees wobble.

I want to twirl on the spot and run back to him. To rest my head against his strong chest, have him wrap me in his arms before he made love to me again and again.

He's my professor but who cares because I've never felt this way before. He's not even that much older than me...I think. My skin tingles from the memory of his fingers tracing my inner thighs, his arousal, his kisses burning me up. To have such a stunning man bring me to orgasm undid me. He broke down my walls, and I gave myself to him completely.

As I remember him buried fully inside me, my body fills with arousal, a feeling that disappears when someone knocks their shoulder into mine so hard, I teeter backward a few steps.

"Watch it, bitch," Clarissa snarls in my face, malice behind her gaze. Others around us stop as if waiting for me to respond, to attack, to do something.

Blinking, I'm waiting for my fogged mind to catch up, to see Clarissa before me, sneering, but I'm in too good a mood to let her or anyone upset me today. Instead, I lower my head and stroll past her and the others.

Someone boos, and I ignore them. Instead, I search for Mercy, hoping she's here since she didn't answer her dorm room when I knocked. But she's nowhere and instead my gaze lands on Alexander who's watching me with a smile from across the room. He's with Finn who stands to throw their rubbish in a nearby trash can.

I stroll toward them, the butterflies in my stomach rebellious against the new emotions crawling through me. Will they be heartbroken to know I had sex with Braxton? Sure, what I have with Alexander and the others is confusing and complicated...still I adore them, and they feel the same way... I am certain. But I'm not ready to raise that conversation with them, not yet.

Mixed feelings twist in my chest. In a heartbeat, everything has changed, somehow making my life even more impossibly confusing.

Alexander pulls a chair closer to him, and I sit down, my cheeks flushing. They shouldn't be, but I experience this sensation like I'm naked and everyone is staring. They see everything and know that I'm hiding a secret.

"Hey, baby," he says and leans in, stealing a quick kiss from my lips that shocks me. He hasn't done something like that before in the cafeteria. "How are you feeling?" His hand is on my thigh, and I glance up into those eyes, blue as the brightest oceans.

My body naturally sways closer to him as if an invisible cord around my chest draws me to him. He always has this effect on me, and my attention fall on his full lips, the color of deep rubies like he's flushed from a jog. He's so beautiful, and in his presence, I always lose myself.

I swallow hard and smile. "A lot better after a long sleep." And sex. My gosh, the sex awakened something inside me, and my whole body is still tingling.

"You okay?" he asks. "You seem different today. Are you still feeling weak from the attack?"

"Different?" I choke out a half laugh, half gasp, then try to remember to breathe.

"Yeah, what's going on Adi?" Finn pipes in from across the table, his feet stretching out to tangle with mine, his grin soft and so dangerously enticing.

"I'm fine. Just had the shock of my life when I found Dixon trying to kill my friend," I answer. "That would freak out anyone." Heat slinks up my back, and I am burning up. Has someone turned up the heat?

"Let me grab you some food. That will help." Finn is on his feet, and I adore how caring they all are, and that makes the guilt inside me worsen. I shouldn't feel guilty because my insides will shatter into a million shards if I lost any of the five guys in my life, but Braxton doesn't exactly get along with Alexander and the others. So, it complicates everything. And what if word got out we slept together. Can Braxton lose his job?

Once Finn strolls toward the food counter, Alexander swivels in his seat to face me, and turns my seat toward him, my legs cradled between his thighs. His hands are on mine, and every touch he delivers comes with heat and intoxicating desire. Keeping my head straight in his presence has always been a problem for me, and it's a hundred times harder today.

"Braxton told me," he began, and my stomach drops through me and all the way to the other side of the planet.

I forget how to breathe, and an icy chill whips through my veins. "He told you?" I squeak, and my cheeks are blushing so incredibly hot, I might pass out. Why would Braxton tell Alexander that we had sex? Was it to gloat or let him know he took my virginity? Right at that moment, I want the world to open up and swallow me, and I can barely hold Alexander's gaze.

I swallow and stare out into the cafeteria, at the mass of people at tables, a few of them looking our way. Did they know too? Who else did Braxton tell?

This has to be a mistake; he wouldn't do that to me. My stomach hurts and I'm going to be sick.

Just then Finn arrives and places a tray filled with a variety of foods. Burger. Fries. Salad. Chicken nuggets. Banana. Two juices, and a small packet of cookies.

"Wasn't sure what you preferred, so I got you a bit of everything," he says, sounding rather proud of himself as he sits down.

But looking at the food makes me want to gag.

The tips of Alexander's finger slip under my chin and he turns my head to him. "Hey, it's going to be okay."

"S-so." I clear my throat, trying to find my voice. "You're okay with it? Not freaking out?"

"It was a little hard to comprehend when I first heard about it, but it's all going to be okay," he answers in a soft voice, a smile spreading over his lips.

"We all feel that way," Finn added.

I turn to him. "You know too?" My arms are trembling, and I want nothing more than to bolt out of there, run and never look anyone in the face. My first time is special, it's a moment I'll cherish forever, not something to be shared on the gossip vine. All I am thinking is bursting to Braxton's office and yelling at him. Or I am misunderstanding?

"We've suspected it for a while," Alexander murmurs.

"You did?" I gasp, getting confused since it just happened recently.

"Well after your attack, and you were in your room for so long with Braxton, I figured it out."

"Figured it out?" I narrow my eyes at him. "You were outside my room, spying?"

His brow furrows into a dozen lines, then exchanges a strange look with Finn before looking back at me. "Did something happen in your room?" It's almost as if he's daring me to say it out loud.

"Did it?" the words slip free, and my glance is flicking between the two men, my heart racing at a million miles an hour.

Finn makes a funny humming sound. "Sounds like something did happen. She's all nervous and twitchy."

"Am not," I insist.

"Is there something you want to tell me?" Alexander asks.

But I can't take this anymore, not knowing exactly what we're talking about, and I can't exactly blurt out, *did you hear me having sex with my teacher?* I'm starting to suspect I might have misunderstood his earlier statement.

Sweat drips down my back, and I'm rubbing my palms down my thighs. "What do you think about what Braxton told you?"

"Not surprised your acting strange in all honesty. It's not easy news to receive."

News to receive. And my mind races right to the precise moment when Braxton explained my blood test and the results of having angel blood in my veins.

I exhale loudly and reach for the pack of cookies before I tear them open. I mean between discussing if I am an angel and if I slept with a teacher to my, I-think-is-my-boyfriend, I'll take angel talk any day of the week.

"Yeah he told me he let you know about the blood tests and apparently being an angel."

I stuffed a small cookie into my mouth whole and chew it slowly as I let my brain catch up to the relief I feel that we weren't talking about sex.

"You seem to be taking it all right," Finn says.

"Well not really sure if I completely buy it, but I'm trying to understand it better. Like if I was an angel, why am I living here and not in heaven? How did I end up with my family? Shouldn't I have wings? And aren't angels assigned to protect and care for someone or something?" I shrug my shoulders. "It's still a bit blurry in my head."

You have angel blood in your veins.

Braxton's words whirl on my mind. He isn't the kind to make up such a lie, but it just can't be true. What would that even mean for me if it was?

Alexander takes my hands in his again, his thumbs gently stroking the back of my hands. "We'll help you through this, explain as much as we can and do research about what we don't know...which is a lot. But you need to understand that no one can find out about this. You'll be in a lot of danger Adi if anyone besides the five of us finds out."

I roll my eyes on reflex. "Right, because someone is going to believe me if I say, hey I'm an angel." Laughter refuses to come, and instead the sound that croaks past my throat is some kind wheezing noise. I gain myself a raised brow from Finn.

"I have so many questions," I admit. "Are there other angels at this school?"

"No," he answers fast. "There hasn't been an angel as far as anyone knows for centuries. Which means that you're going to be wanted by many who'd harm you. Which is why you need to let us protect you. One of us will always be with you from now on."

I shiver. "Who'd want an angel and what for?"

Something raw lashes over Alexander's gaze, and my question surprises him.

But he doesn't need to answer. I picture Mercy in my head, Dixon on top of her, draining energy out of her. "Dixon isn't human, is he?" I ask, narrowing my eyes at Alexander then Finn.

They both shake their heads. "So what is he? A demon? And what about Mercy... is she something too, is this whole school for non-humans? I mean how else would you guys and Braxton even know I was an angel and act so casually about it." My words are rolling out fast, and my brain is buzzing with so many unknowns. And if someone dangerous is after me, I have to know everything.

"She's human," Finn explains.

But someone catches my attention from across the cafeteria. Connor is staring at me, his brow pinched together with disapproval. His words about not trusting anyone or the teachers plays on my thoughts. Does he know something about angels? I've known him for years at my old school and he's never said anything like that to me before. I hadn't noticed anything out of the ordinary about him then to lead me to believe he was something beyond human either.

"I know this is overwhelming," Finn murmurs. "But it might be easier to first accept you're an angel and then we can slowly answer more questions. How does that sound?"

My response about it not being easier for me is swallowed by the bell ringing. I glance up. "What's going on?" I ask.

"Movie night. You want to join us?" Alexander asks. "Might be a good distraction."

But I shake my head without asking what movie they're showing. I'm not in the right head space to concentrate on anything. So much has happened today that it's hurting my head. "I think I'll have an early night."

"Okay, I'll wait until you finish your dinner and I'll walk you back to your room," Alexander says while staring at Finn, and a silent conversation is going on between their stares.

"I'm going to meet up with Nyx and Dante, and we'll see you tomorrow." Finn stands and walks over to my side. He leans in closer and kisses me ever so lightly, his fingers grazing over my arm, eliciting a wave of heat traveling over my skin. "You have no idea how glad I am that you're alright, pretty girl," he whispers in my ear. Everything about these guys has my body reacting from their sweet words to their perfect looks. I take a deep breath, forcing my body to relax as he walks away, and I try to eat something to fill my empty stomach. After half a burger and a few fries, I grab the fruit off my tray, and I walk with Alexander back to my room.

Outside my door, I turn to face Alexander. One hand pressed to the doorframe, he reaches over and pushes back caught at the corner of my mouth. "Everything will be alright. Nothing will harm you. We'll do anything to keep you safe."

I believe him, having no reason not to, but I need to figure some of this out for my sanity and safety. I've learned the hard way in life not to be wholly dependent on people.

Everything is so complicated. I'm exhausted, and I'm having trouble absorbing everything that's happened today, so I'm hoping sleep will recharge my brain.

"Do you want me to stay with you?" he asks, his hand cupping my cheek. I lean into his touch, drawn to him more than ever.

I consider his question, heat surging over my body at the idea of having him in my room, staying the night. I almost roll my eyes at myself. I've finally had sex for the first time and here I am contemplating having a second guy in my bed in the same week. Okay, maybe I am jumping to conclusions that he would want that, but I'm not thinking straight right now.

My lips part. "I'd love that more than you know," I whisper, keeping the conversation between us low and hidden from anyone walking past the hall, glancing our way.

"I feel a but coming," he says, and his wonky, cute smile makes me laugh.

I should have said good night and walked into my room, but instead I reach out and run my fingertips through his thick, black hair. He presses closer, his body flush with mine and his forehead rests against mine. My breaths are racing, and I forget myself when I'm this close to Alexander.

"You're so beautiful, so special to me, Adi. More than you'll ever know." His mouth lowers to mine and kisses me, his affection caressing my heart. He parts my lips and takes my tongue into his mouth, and my stomach is bursting with butterflies beating their wings in excitement. In those few moments when I'm lost to him, I kiss him back with everything I have. With passion. With desire, With love.

"Good night, Adi," he finally says against my mouth as he pulls away, leaving me utterly breathless.

His devious smirk tells me he knows exactly what he's doing, teasing me because I didn't invite him into my room. He's playing a game.

So, I tilt my head back, run my tongue over my lower lip slowly, drawing his attention, and I turn to open my door.

When I glance back over my shoulder, I see the hunger in Alexander's eyes, the way he stares at me like he's fighting himself to hold back from taking what he wants...from taking me.

"Good night," I say.

"Be careful." His words stay with me as I shut the door and lock it. I press my back to the door, buzzing all over from that incredible kiss. Closing my eyes, I force myself to slow my breaths.

Be careful.

My mind is overthinking everything, and I can't work out if he's talking about danger or what he may do to me if I keep teasing him. Slipping my lip between my teeth, I gnaw on the flesh and I pray with everything in me he's referring to the latter.

CHAPTER 4

*T*he next morning, the sun is out from behind the heavy clouds that always stain the skies over the Academy. I take that as a good omen for today because after the recent discovery of Mercy and Dixon, things can't get worse. With the exception of the sex yesterday that is...that wasn't the worse.

The whole night I stirred in and out of broken sleep. My mind refusing to stop racing. But now that my head is clear, I have every intention of finding out what is going on. I pull out my journal and start jotting down everything I've been thinking.

The things I know for certain are:

- I'm apparently an angel. Okay, I am still a bit sketchy on the details but curious if this is some cruel joke, making me look like a fool. Please don't let it be that as it'll break me into so many pieces after my day with Braxton yesterday. Braxton and Alexander both seem to agree on the whole angel thing, which scares me because what if it's true? I can't even fathom what that means. Yep, I'm completely messed up whichever direction this goes.
- Dixon isn't human. So what is he? He was feeding on Mercy,

that much I can tell. But what was he feeding on? What was the white mist?

- Who the heck are my real parents if I am an angel? (See first note.)
- Connor knows something and I intend to find out more from him. He owes me.
- Yesterday I lost my virginity. I feel I need to add this on the list because I had sex with a teacher and I want to tell someone how the moment is forever imprinted on my brain, has me panting for air, and feels like my body is catching alight everything I think about it. Every touch from Braxton still tingles over my skin, every kiss was filled with adoration that makes it seems like he really does love me.
- Alexander and the others don't know I had sex with Braxton, and after the kiss with Alexander last night, I don't want to lose any of them if they find out about my sexy times and feel betrayed. So, this last point is to not bring up the topic ever if possible. Also, does this make me the worst person ever that I want all of them?

Already, I'm hyperventilating so I push those thoughts to the farthest recesses of my mind, closing my notebook and stuffing it in my drawer before I go mad.

I need to see Mercy.

And with that thought, a strange peace settles over me. I push my legs out of bed and hurry to get ready for the day.

The hallway is silent today, my footfalls hitting on the stone floor as I hurry toward Mercy's room.

Three knocks and finally the door opens.

My heart is banging loudly against my ribcage.

Mercy greets me with a crooked smile, her eyes puffy like she's been crying.

"Mercy." I move to hug her and drag her into my arms as she cries softly against my shoulder, and it breaks my heart to see her in so much agony. I can't help but think this has everything to do with Dixon's attack.

My gaze drifts over her shoulder and into the room, half expecting to find someone in the room with her, except she's alone. The window I'd seen shattered is now completely fixed without a sign that her ex had hurled himself through the glass.

"I'm okay," she admits while sniffling and sounding defeated before turning and walking deeper into her dorm.

My stomach twists.

On her heels, I enter the room, only to find two suitcases on the bed filled with clothes and books and shoes and her laptop. Only then do I look around the room.

Looking around, I see that it's barren of all her belongings. I turn back to look at her frantically. "What are you doing, Mercy?"

She slouches on the edge of the bed, hands on her lap, and a pained look across her face. "I'm leaving Raven Academy. I was going to come and see you before I left."

Shock knives cleanly through me that I'll lose the only true friend I have in this academy...maybe the only true friend I've ever had. She's the person who has stood up for me when everyone targeted me, she's made me laugh...she's made me feel like I belong. Now, I can barely breathe as my fears are realized. The fear that I'll be all alone.

Trying desperately to draw in my disappointment, I cross the room in two steps and sit next to her so close our legs and arms are touching. I offer her a shaky smile.

"Because of the attack?" I ask.

Clenching her fists, she sighs heavily and pushes off the bed. "I can only recall bits and pieces of what happened, but I remember seeing Dixon attacking you. And I know that my ex was in the room too."

I shiver remembering Dixon lunging at me, and the hairs on my nape lift.

"It's one thing for me to be a target, but he attacked you because of me. I should have let you tell someone about him. I just can't stay here anymore," she chokes the words out and wipes at the tears threading down her cheeks.

I take her hand in mine. "This isn't your fault, Mercy."

She swings toward me, taking her hand back. "I saw what he did, I saw him dragging your limp body into the room before he..." she gasps and looks away, her shoulders shaking from the cries wracking her body.

"Before he did what? Drank my energy, or whatever the hell he was doing to you?"

"No." She whirls back to face me again, drying her eyes with the back of her hand. "He was pulling your skirt up to rape you, Adi. To fucking rape you as he fed on you." Her words are like a punch to my chest.

That fucking bastard. I'm shaking all over as an image of him over me on the floor assaults my mind.

"Did he do it? Did he try raping you too?" I whisper with a shaky voice, my skin crawling with the thought.

She's shaking her head and relief crashes through me. "No, he never has that I can remember. But thank god, Connor burst into the room and they got into a huge brawl. I passed out after that and then woke up in the nurse's office early this morning. After I found out you were okay, I made the decision to leave. And maybe you should do the same, Adi. Something's wrong here. Something evil is in these walls."

"Connor saved us both?" I don't know why but hearing it was him surprises me.

Mercy's words carry the same trepidation as Connor's when he warned me about not trusting anyone. My emotions are swinging like a pendulum between the monsters in this school to the way my heart flutters for the five men who've captivated me. And leaving them seems impossible. An ache settles deep in my stomach to the point of nausea at the thought of leaving them.

"It's my fault, Adi, and I can't do this anymore." More tears fall and she shuts her bags, zipping up her belongings before she tugs the suitcases off the bed.

What am I supposed to say? Stay when it's clear she's terrified and in danger? A tremble skitters down my spine. "Will you keep in touch?"

Instead of answering me, she leaps into my arms and she's crying, full on bawling her eyes out. I hold her tight, and my eyes are tearing up again at hearing the agony tearing through her. Sorrow creeps into my heart, and my throat swells with the strongest desire to cry. I don't want my friend to leave but asking her to stay is purely selfish on my part.

There's a long pause before she pulls from my arms and breaks into a half chuckle. "I must look like a mess."

"You look perfect." I find a sliver of courage to smile.

She takes a deep breath and nods. "I better go. Dad is picking me up from reception any minute now."

"Come, I'll help you." I reach out with an unsteady hand and take one of her bags on wheels and roll it out of her room.

My chest is burning up, and I quickly wipe the hot tears escaping from the corner of my eyes at the thought of losing my friend. But I don't want her to see me like this and feel worse.

"Message me every day," she says, and I nod.

"You better do the same. I want daily updates on what school you go to, if you find any hotties, and photos."

Her mouth curls upward with the mischievous look on her face I've grown used to seeing every day. "You want me to take photos of hot guys without being seen? A bit stalkerish, but doable."

"I'm going to miss you so much, Mercy. Even your crazy conspiracy theories."

"I'm going to miss seeing your gorgeous face so much."

There are so many things I want to tell her, to confess somehow how conflicted I'm feeling. How the guys think I'm an angel, how I had freaking sex with my teacher. But I hold all those words and feelings back. This isn't a moment about me but about Mercy doing what she needs for her sanity.

By the time we reach reception, she's half bouncing on her toes like leaving has been on her mind for longer than just after this incident and she's desperate to get out of here now that she's so close to escape.

A tall man in tailored pants and a white business shirt waits near the reception, talking to the principal.

"Dad," Mercy calls out, her voice wavering, clear she's missed her parents. It reminds me of mine and how much I want to see them. But I also remember that the reason I'm here is to help pay for Dad's medical costs, and I'll stay here for as long as it takes if Dad heals from the sickness wracking through his body.

Both men turn toward us, and Mercy's dad's eyes light up at seeing his daughter. He strolls over and takes her into his arms.

I'll lie if I say I'm not jealous at seeing them. It just makes me miss my parents desperately, to hear his words that everything will be alright. I can't tell them about anything going on at the academy though or they'll force me to return home despite needing the help for Dad's health bills. And for that reason, I'll stay here and will make it work somehow.

"Let me take your bags to the car. I'm parked just outside." Her dad offers me a gentle smile, and I see the similarities. Same almond-shaped eyes. Both wearing dark framed glasses, and there are small waves in his short hair, just like Mercy's curls.

She turns to me as her dad takes her bags.

We hug for the longest moment, and I try to remember how it feels to have her hold me so hard I can barely breathe, how she always smells of lavender and sandalwood, and how I'll no longer have my friend by my side.

"Well, I better go," she says as she breaks away. "I'll be in touch, and please, Adi." She lowers her voice. "Be careful. This school is a lot more dangerous than it seems."

People keep telling me that but when her gaze softens like she might cry again and she doesn't even know half of it, I squeeze her arm. "You better go before your dad comes searching for you," I joke, but in truth, I'm struggling to hold myself together.

She walks away, her curls bouncing over her shoulders, reminding me of the first time we met in the girls' toilets where I hid from Clarissa. We shared a common element... we were outcasts but fighters.

41

Now, tears are running down my cheeks. A pang of guilt washes over me that she left because of me.

I turn and run to my room. There I'm pacing back and forth, the wrath of my emotions pulsing through me, and I let myself cry hard. Anything to stop the pain of losing a friend on a day I was convinced would be a new start.

Dropping onto the bed, I bury my face into a pillow and have no idea how much time passes before I finally roll onto my back, my eyes stinging from the endless crying.

I am going to miss her dearly, and there is nothing I can do to change her leaving.

Standing, I reach for my phone in my pocket and dial home.

It goes to the voicemail, and I sigh, half contemplating to hang up, but I don't.

"Hey Mom and Dad, it's me. Just calling to see how you're both doing. Wanted to hear your voices. How are Dad's new medicines working? Anyway, I miss you and I'll try to call again later. Love you." I hang up and instead of moping around any longer, I get up and grab my toiletries before I head to the bathroom to apply as much foundation and makeup as needed to hide my puffy eyes and not show the world I've been crying all morning.

* * *

THE FIRST FEW classes of the day pass in a blur and I do my best to concentrate on the lessons, thinking endlessly about Mercy leaving. Heaviness surges through me and over lunch, I can barely stomach my meal, so I push my chicken tenders away.

"Not hungry?" Nyx takes the seat across from me in the food hall and gives me the sweetest smile that eases the sorrow riveting through me.

I adore the way he looks at me like all the people and noise around him don't distract him and it's only me he sees. He reaches over and runs a thumb over my cheek. "There's so much sadness in your eyes today, gorgeous. What's going on?"

I'm biting my lip in concentration, glancing up at him and the words spill out. "Mercy left Raven Academy today. She's gone back home."

Looking down, I blink hard to bat the tears away. I don't want to cry again, not in front of everyone or Nyx. "I just miss her so much."

His hand slides across my back, his touch captivating, his fingers rubbing the small of my back in small circles as he shuffles closer. "I'm sorry, baby girl. I heard about the attack and I've been looking for you to find out how you are."

"I'm dealing. I'm more upset about losing my friend to be honest." Mercy's words came to me about Dixon, and I swivel in my seat to face Nyx, those pale blue eyes are striking against the thickest, darkest lashes. His deep brown hair looks ruffled and I reach out to tame down a few wild strands on his head.

He catches my wrist and brings it to his lips. I'm buzzing all over at how gently he kisses along my palm and the tip of each finger. "I'm so sorry we weren't there faster to stop that bastard from touching you."

I naturally push myself closer to him and he kisses me deeply. Just a heartbeat of a kiss, but enough to leave me fluttering on the inside as an overwhelming surge of desire sweeps through me. Already I feel a little better.

"He won't touch you again, my little angel."

I meet his gaze; well aware his angel comment has everything to do with him agreeing with everyone else that I'm an angel. I want to believe and accept that because maybe then I will have the power to somehow bring more love to this world, to stop those like Dixon and Clarissa from ever attacking others again.

Nyx is on his feet and pulling me by a hand to join him. "Come with me."

My body moves, obeying his request, reeling me toward him, and I don't resist him because I want to be with him.

We traipse down the hall and outside where the morning sun had slipped behind heavy clouds that now darken the sky. A cold wind blows through my hair. Nyx holds me against him, and we're moving with haste across the lawn.

"Where are we going?" I ask.

"I want to show you something."

His words intrigue me, and there's something exciting with how he wants to surprise me. I settle against him and we fall into a rhythm of steps, making our way past all the buildings and to the rear of the school grounds. Trees crowd closer here, shadows dancing amid the trunks, and the grass grows wild. Up ahead is an old rundown four story building, charred black like it had been burned.

"I've never been here before."

"It's the original school building where all the classes used to be held. But a huge fire broke out after something went wrong in a science class, and the powers to be never rebuilt it."

"Did anyone get hurt?"

"Not sure." We move closer to the building, trampling over the long grass, and we step through the front opening where the doors are lying on the ground. A lock and chains are smashed and tossed aside on the ground in front of us, rusted from long ago.

The place is gutted, with no furniture or decorations. Just the walls charred black, ash and dirt littering the ground, the ceiling peeling.

The smell is rancid and carries with it a burning smell. "It stinks in here."

"Yeah, but it's worth it, I promise."

He pulls me quickly toward the stone staircase, and we rush upstairs, past the animal droppings. Up on the top floor, the hallway is dark and there's a terrifying zombie-vibe going on here.

"This place is freaky. Where did you say we're going again?"

"I didn't but you can trust me." His grip slightly squeezes my hand, and I trust him completely as he takes me down a hall then through the fire escape door, and up more stairs.

Finally, he pushes a door open and bright light from outside beams over me. I squint and step outside onto the flat roof where there are plastic chairs and tables set up, a few trashcans, and even several strings of fairy lights cross over our heads. The place looks cleaned up, showing no sign of the fire that has swallowed the rest of the building.

"Is this place used for parties?" How come I don't know about this spot?

Nyx is at my back, his arms looping around my stomach, his mouth on my neck, leaving a trail of kisses up to my ear.

Heat rises through me, and my skin ripples with excitement. I'm at his mercy, softening against his chest.

"This isn't what I came to show you."

He turns me on the spot slowly and walks me to the side of the building. We pause feet from the edge made of a small lip. Below is a straight drop to my death. Shivers grip me. I've never loved heights, and up here, the wind is blustering against me. It feels like I'm on the edge of the world. My heart is in my throat and I try to step backward, but Nyx holds me in place.

"I've got you." His hold tightens, a playful tone in his voice. "Now look straight ahead for me."

I reassure myself I'm safe and he won't let anything happen to me. The cool air calms me as does Nyx's arms that hold me in place. I lift my gaze and stare out over the tops of the forest that encases Raven Academy and into the distance where white water cascades down from a cliff's edge and rocky outcrops, giving the impression that there are multiple waterfalls. The sun in that area seems to hit the water at the right angel, creating a rainbow arching over the river.

"Wow. I didn't know that existed so close to us."

"It's gorgeous isn't it?"

I'm mesmerized, and I hold onto Nyx's arms, not from fear of falling, but the contentment washing over me.

"This is insanely beautiful," I say, smiling over my shoulder at him. "It's perfect."

"No one comes here during the day, so I sit here when I want time away from everything, when things feel like too much."

"I appreciate you sharing your hideaway with me. That means a lot to me." I can't stop staring at the beauty of the falling water, at how divine nature is. It reminds me that the simplicity of life in the face of something so powerful.

"You're welcome to join me here anytime. It can be our secret place."

Nodding, I turn in his arms to face him, and soft prickles dance over my flesh, my breaths racing. Somehow amid the chaos around me, Nyx has found a way to help me find peace in my heart.

With us so close now, all I can think of is the hardness of his body against mine, and I draw my eyes up to meet his.

"I've wanted to bring you here for a while," he explains, but my breaths are caught in my chest as I study how incredibly handsome he is from those perfect lips calling to me, to the sharp cheekbones, and the faint shade of stubble along his jawline.

His hands splay across my back and he pulls me against his solid chest for a kiss. I grip onto his strong arms, rising myself on tippy toes. His tongue surges into my mouth, and I take him, taste him, give myself to him. A soft moan slips from my throat, and his grasp tightens around my back.

"You have no idea what you do to me, Adi," he groans into my mouth, staring at me intently.

I press myself closer to the mass bulk of him, nestling close, embracing him. He holds me, and we stay like that for a while, I needed a hug more than I realize. I don't want to let him go or leave this place, ever. My heart beats steadily, and we hold each other while the world fades around us. There's something special about a quiet moment without the distraction of words but knowing I'm not alone.

It isn't long before the school bell shatters the peace to announce the end of lunch.

Nyx pulls away, his hand sliding into mine, our fingers intertwining. "Should take you back," he announces, and I sigh in protest.

He laughs in response, and I adore the sound so much that I let myself just stand there and watch how incredibly gorgeous he is, how the lines at the corners of his eyes crease, how he throws his head back slightly, how his hands gently draw me closer. Everything about him, about this moment is so perfect. I capture it in my mind, store it away for when the world feels like it's going to hell around me.

I take his hand and he walks me back. "I'm definitely getting you to keep your word and bring me back here," I say.

"I don't doubt it for a moment, and that was my plan. Up here no one will hear your sweet moans." He looks at me with so much desire in his eyes and hunger, that I can't stop the blush from creeping over my face.

"I have so many more things I want to show you," he adds as he sees me back to class, and all I can think is that somehow I've let myself fall for five guys, given my heart to each and I worry that somehow I'll end up heartbroken and devastated. My worst fear is I'll end up losing all of them.

The rest of the day flies by and I keep wondering how I can sneak dinner to my room and eat myself into a coma to forget how much I miss Mercy.

Out in the hallway as I leave a classroom, I join the masses to make our way toward the dorms, when someone grabs my arm and yanks me out of the river of students.

I stumble on my feet and twirl around just as Clarissa shoves me backward and into an empty hallway.

My hackles rise at seeing her in my face.

"Well, well, well," she murmurs, her hand shoving into my shoulders, sending me reeling backward until my back finds the wall. "We get you're a whore and sleeping with half the school, so you don't need to parade it in our faces while we're trying to eat. It's sickening, and you know everyone is talking about you, right? How many more guys are you going to add to your harem? Ten. Twenty?"

Her words startle me until I remember my quick kiss with Nyx in the food hall. She must have been watching me, hating me with the same loathing and jealousy lashing over her gaze right now.

"Leave me the hell alone, Clarissa, I don't have time for you." I go to move, but she pushes me back.

She snorts in a gasp of air. "It's funny that you think you can get away from me, bitch. I'm the shadow you can never escape."

I can't help myself and burst out laughing. "Is that supposed to scare me? Who even says things like that?"

She lunges at me, coming so fast, I don't react quick enough. She jams her forearm up against my throat, driving me back, holding me still. She's so freaky strong and fast, and threads of fear coil in my gut.

I shove my hands against her, but she doesn't budge.

"Why do you think Mercy really left? Because you ignored her to get yourself dick! You're a bitch and a shit friend and soon enough even the guys will tire of you. Then you can crawl back into whatever hole you came from and die."

Her malicious words are a blade to my heart, and they shouldn't affect me because she's lying, I know that, but my stomach is clenching and I'm dying a little on the inside. Did Mercy really think I picked the guys over her?

"Fuck you!" my words tremble and I hate that I'm showing her the effect she has on me.

She laughs and releases me. "No thanks. Pretty sure you have enough guys doing that already."

I grit my jaw, refusing to let her get the better of me as I rub my sore neck. I remember something I read online on good comebacks and the words fall out of my mouth. "You don't like me? That's a shame. I'll pencil in some time to cry about it later."

Her eyes widen just enough for me to see she isn't a fan and I offer her a grin. "What your back, bitch." With a flick of red hair over her shoulder, she strolls away and merges into the stream of students in the main hall.

I collapse against the wall, shaking and furious that I let her treat me this way. I should have ripped her hair out or something. I feel like I'm back to day one of attending this school, and I'm the target practice. I want to crawl under a rock and hide because somehow today is worse than yesterday. And the excitement from my first time with Braxton, plus the beautiful moment with Nyx are ruined with Clarissa's ugly words circling my mind.

I hate her.

I hate her more than I should despise anyone.

I turn and push myself into a fast walk out of the building, chin tucked into my chest, I hug myself and run. But I feel them staring... all the eyes, everyone judging me.

Everyone is talking about you.

That's all I hear the whole way back to my dorm, and I shut myself inside my room swallowed by the desperation to follow Mercy's footsteps and leave this place.

CHAPTER 5

*W*ild thoughts are running crazily through my head as I lay in bed on Saturday morning. Thoughts of doing something other than sitting in my room all weekend, leaving the campus, going somewhere other than Raven Academy run through my mind. A change of scenery might be good, and I wonder if anyone will notice if I sneak off the grounds and go to a movie, shopping, something that feels normal. Maybe take a break from dealing with killings and confusing emotions.

And what I wouldn't give for a vanilla chai tea latte.

When my phone rings, I scramble out of bed, hoping it's Mercy. Except it's someone even better, and I hit the answer button.

"Mom! How are you?" At the back of my mind, I remind myself of what I've discovered about my blood type and that in truth they aren't my real parents. I don't want to think about that when all I need is some happiness for a little while.

"Hi sweetie," she says, and I hear the smile in her voice. It sounds happier than it has in a long time. "How's school going?"

I shrug even though she can't see me. "It's okay. One of my friends left this week, so I'm missing her."

In Mom's background, it sounds almost windy. "That's horrible," she adds. "But we have a surprise that might cheer you up."

"Really, what is it?" The sound grows louder. "Where are you? It's so loud around you."

"We spoke to your principal and he's given you permission to come up for the weekend."

I rock on my feet and squeal as Mom groans at how loud it sounds in her ears. "Are you serious, Mom, because this isn't funny if it's a joke."

"Of course it's true. Dad's at home making his famous pot roast for you."

I'm bouncing on my feet. "You're on your way here now?"

"Just pulling into the driveway."

"Oh my god, give me ten and I'm out there! I love you so much, Mom." I hang up and squeal to my heart's delight, then rush like a mad person to pack a small bag, grab my clothes and rush to the bathroom for the world's fastest shower.

I'm running like a mad woman toward reception, smiling crazily when Dante turns the corner toward me, strolling with hands deep in the pockets of his jeans, looking so incredibly delicious in jeans sitting low on his hips and a white t-shirt, loosely tucked in. Loose strands of golden hair sit over one eye as he closes in, strolling lazily in a way that has me pausing and admiring him. My heart races out of my chest. I see the way he stares at me, and it takes me a moment to remember to breathe.

Longing. Burning. Heat.

"Hey, babe, what's the rush?" he eyes the backpack hanging off a shoulder. "Where are you going?"

"Mom's taking me home for the weekend. I can't wait to see them." My words are rushing with excitement.

Dante smiles, but I see the disappointment behind his eyes. "Sounds amazing. My plans for taking you on a picnic today will have to wait."

"Picnic? I love that idea."

"Guess someone else will have to eat those homemade oatmeal chocolate chip cookies."

"What, you baked them for me? Those are my favorite!"

He shrugs with a devious smile that works to melt me. "Might have been a one-off thing."

I playfully slap him on the arm. "Don't you dare. I need to taste your cookies."

He arches a brow and smirks so sexily; it makes me blush.

"You're saying you want to reschedule our picnic then?"

Warmth is washing all over me. He has this effect on me with his charming, broody personality coupled with a mountain of sexiness.

He leans closer, and my stomach flutters at being so close to him, at inhaling his sexy scent. I stare into those golden eyes, at his parted lips like he might kiss me, and my mouth tingles as he inches even closer.

Instead, he reaches for my bag and takes it off my shoulder to carry it for me before chuckling. "Come, I'll walk with you so you're not keeping your parents waiting."

I sulk. "You're such a tease, you know that." I force myself to stay calm, but before we reach the next corner, I turn to him, fist his shirt over his chest and pull him toward me.

Our mouths clash, and my body is burning up like a supernova. Tearing down through earth's atmosphere scorching hotter by the second.

He drops my bag by our feet and collects me into his arms, pressing us so close that our bodies intertwine. He kisses me back full of passion, and it feels perfectly right. His fingers sink into the softness of my ass.

We pull back, I'm gasping for breath, face flashed. His eyes are wild with desire.

"Just a little something to remember to make some of those cookies," I tease, an evil grin pulling at my lips. Still, a fiery passion burns right down to my core.

Dante's staring at me with intensity like he forgot to breathe just then, his eyes devouring all of me. Then he shakes his head like he's trying to wake up from his own fantasy, and I won't deny it feels incredible to get such a reaction from a gorgeous man.

He licks his lips like a lion. "When you return." He clears his throat. "I may have to change our picnic plans a bit."

"I'm looking forward to it." I take deep breaths and try to calm myself as electric fire covers me. Maybe kissing him so deeply was a mistake before meeting with my mom. Except around Dante and the others, I completely lose myself.

He picks up my bag and we resume our walk, both of us stealing glances and smiling. It's funny how even with the smallest connection the guys who hold my heart can help lift my spirits higher than I thought possible.

Our pace is even as we make our way to the front foyer near the reception, and I find Mom waiting near the door.

She rushes over to me, her eyes wide as is her smile, and I hug her so hard, I forgot how good it feels, how she always smells of clementines.

"Adeline, I've missed you so much," she whispers then breaks away. She still holds my hands, staring at me like I might have changed since she last saw me. "You look taller and more mature."

"You can tell that?"

But her attention swings to Dante who stands near me. I reach over and take my bag from his grasp. "Mom, this is Dante. Dante, this is my Mom."

"It's a pleasure to meet you, Mrs. Jones." He gives a slight bow of his head.

"Nice to meet you. Glad Adeline's made some friends. She definitely needs more friends." She keeps emphasizing the word friends, and I'm about to die.

"Mom." I roll my eyes. "Let's go."

She laughs softly. "Well nice to meet you, Dante." She turns to leave, and I glance over at Dante, mouthing, *Sorry*.

He blows me a kiss, which melts my knees, and I rush after Mom out of the building to an overcast day. The wind is warm today, and it isn't long before we're buckled up in the car and driving home.

"Dante seems nice," Mom begins, and I recognize the soft prying tone where she's dying to ask if he's my boyfriend but won't say it.

"Yeah, he's great," I reply.

She cuts me a look with narrowing eyes. "That's it? A spunk like that carries your bag for you, and that's all you give me?"

"Spunk? Is that from the eighties? No one talks like that."

She laughs at me and turns on the radio. "As long as he treats you well and doesn't distract your studies, and most importantly, you don't let him into your dorm room, then it's okay."

"Mom!" I practically screech, thinking of her reaction if she found out that I had just lost my virginity to my professor.

She reaches over and pats my thigh. "I've missed you so much."

"So much." I exhale a deep breath. "You have no clue how happy it makes me that I get to spend a weekend at home."

"Okay, so tell me everything about Raven Academy."

I spend the long trip giving her details on classes, teachers, the dragon statues, the meals we get, and even how much fun the camping trip was despite the disastrous ending. I leave out the obvious boyfriend situation and killings and bullying. I don't want to worry them or create any reason for them to take me from the school and risk Dad no longer having his medical bills paid.

As we pull up in the driveway, there's something almost surreal to stare up at our house. Somehow it looks older, smaller.

We climb out and I grab my bag from the back seat. Without waiting for Mom who's opening the garage door seeing as they still haven't fixed the broken remote control, I rush inside and dump my bag near the door.

"Dad," I call out and hurry down the open foyer and toward the kitchen toward the back of the house.

He's not there, so I step to the back door and look outside to find him in our small garden, holding a bunch of fresh herbs. My heart soars at seeing him out and about a bit, and he looks so much better. More color in his face.

I palm open the door and rush outside, my feet sinking into the soft lawn.

Dad turns to me, his mouth curls into a smile, and he steps my way. I run to him and hug him tight, my head snuggled against his chest. His arms go around my back and he kisses the top of my head.

He feels skinnier in my embrace, thickening my throat, but I put on a brave face and look up at him. "Can you tell I've missed you?"

"If sending you away was all it took to make you hug me this much, I would have sent you to a boarding school ages ago," he jokes.

"Yeah right. So how are you doing, what did the doctors say? Tell me everything." I can't wait for another moment. I want to hear the words that his prostate cancer is gone, and he no longer needs chemo.

"Treatments have worked incredibly well. I got a call from the doctor this morning who said all signs of the cancer are gone. A few more treatments to be sure, and I'll be diagnosed as in remission. I can finally grow all my hair back." He runs a hand over his bald head, but I don't notice anything but the joy in his smile, the cheeriness in his voice. I can hear the positiveness in his words, all the stress is gone. The stress of not having enough money to pay for the treatments and medication. The stress of his sickness.

Tears are pushing forward and I wish they wouldn't because this is fantastic news. But Dad catches one of my tears as it runs down my cheek. "Don't cry for me. The doctor said it was miraculous how quickly I've healed, and it's all because you made the sacrifice to go to Raven Academy."

"I'd go and live on the moon if it meant you'd heal, and you never died." Saying the word had my chin quivering and the tears falling heavy. Tears for the sorrow for my dad I've been bravely holding onto, the fear that I'd lose him.

"Oh, baby, come here." He took me into his arms and held me as I let it all out. I didn't realize how much I've been holding onto until now.

"She finally comes home, and you make her cry?" Mom calls out from the back door.

Dad's laughing and rubbing my back until I turn around and wipe my eyes dry.

"Did you tell your dad about your boyfriend?"

I almost die at hearing her gloating.

"What? Who? I need to know and see if he's good enough for Adeline," he jokes, and it feels amazing to hear him so happy. The heaviness in the house before I left for Raven Academy weighed on me, but now it feels full of promise and love.

"Oh, not a boyfriend. He's just some guy I met." Not like I can admit I might have four boyfriends, plus a teacher I lost my virginity too, and oh yes, I'm having strange feelings toward Connor again. When I think of it that way, Clarissa's words float in my head. But I shake them off, refusing to bring her negativity with me.

"He's super sweet and so kind. He was planning on taking me on a picnic today."

"And you turned him down for us?"

"Of course, are you mad? Family always comes first. Isn't that what you used to say?"

"Good girl." he swings an arm around my shoulders, and we stroll back toward the house. This is exactly what I need to rebalance myself and get my thoughts straight about everything going on back at the Academy.

* * *

I STUFF another mouthful of Dad's beef roast into my mouth, the salty, spicy flavor engulfing my tastebuds. The meat melts on my tongue. "This is so good." I cut another piece and don't stop eating until my plate is empty.

Dad's already slicing more and filling my plate again, while I scoop the baked potatoes and carrots onto my plate as well.

"I thought you said you ate lots at school," Dad says. "No wonder you're looking a bit skinny."

"Yeah, but it doesn't taste like home cooking." I glance up at my parents sitting across from me at the kitchen table, smiling and chatting like the old days. On the fridge farther behind Mom is a photo of the three of us next to a donkey from a couple of years ago. We'd gone on a trip to the Grand Canyon and we all rode a donkey down the steep terrain.

I love my parents unconditionally, but the memory of my blood test has been floating in my mind most of the day. To ask them about the truth, where I came from. Maybe that will help me work out the whole angel theory.

Chewing on my food, I twirl the words in my thoughts on how to ask. Blurt it out, hint at it, make a joke about being adopted?

"You're looking very serious," Dad murmurs. "What's going on in that pretty head of yours?"

I grab my glass of apple juice and wash down the food in my mouth and try to calm my bouncing knees under the table. "They made us have blood tests at school." My heart twists, and I want to swallow but my mouth goes suddenly dry, so I finish my juice.

Mom and Dad exchange knowing looks, and I see the panic crawling over their faces. They know what I'm referring to, I see it scribbled all over their furrowing expressions.

Maybe I shouldn't have said anything, maybe I should have waited a bit longer. I don't want Dad to worry, and now I regret saying anything, at least until after Dad has the all clear from the doctors.

With a deep breath, Mom places her fork down on the table and turns toward me. "Think it's about time we show you something." She rose to her feet, while Dad wipes his mouth and gets up as well.

Trepidation slithers through me at what they'll show me, and I follow them up to their bedroom. I sit on the edge of the queen-sized bed, while Dad opens the wardrobe and reaches deep on the top shelf. He pulls out a tiny box and both my parents sit on the bed across from me.

Dad opens the wooden box, the hinges making a tiny squeak.

With a deep breath I look inside.

Dad pulls out a dusty pink ribbon and he lays it across my open palm. It's as thick as my index finger and as long as my hand. My name has been carefully embroidered into the fabric, the stitching delicate and tiny. Dad places a white feather in my hand alongside the ribbon. It's silky to the touch, and I look up at him with confusion.

C.R. JANE & MILA YOUNG

"What does this mean?" The anxiety is strangling me as I keep staring from the feather to my parents.

"Your mom and I have never been able to have children, and we'd been praying for years."

Mom shuffles closer and takes my hand, a thin smile lingers on her mouth, her eyes watery. "One night we found you on our doorstep in a basket. That ribbon was tied to your wrist, and the feather tangled inside your messy blonde hair." She pushes my hair off my face and cups my cheek. "You were so adorable with round, rosy cheeks, crystal blue eyes, and you never cried. You were the perfect baby as if God himself delivered you to us."

I can't help but think how ironic her words are about God, when all I can hear in my head is Braxton telling me I might be an angel.

I don't say anything for a bit as I try to process everything.

"My real parents just abandoned me then. Is something wrong with me?" My voice is tight.

"Baby." Mom drew me into her arms, hugging me, covering me in kisses. "Don't think like that. You were meant to be with us, that's what matters. Some people can't cope with a young child." Her words fade away. "You were almost one when you came to us."

Then she sniffles. I hug her back, and I notice Dad is watching us with a glassy gaze.

I have so many questions as I look down at the feather clenched in my hand, remembering the blood test at school.

You have angel blood.

I don't mention to my parents the angel idea as I worry they'll think I've gone mad. And with Mom softly sobbing against me and Dad moving over to hug us both, I'm barely holding on myself. Plus, if they found me on their doorstep, what else can they know?

"Sorry you had to find out this way," Dad rasps. "We wanted to tell you but never found the right moment."

"I love you both, and no matter what, you're my parents," I say, never taking my eyes off the feather. Unsure how much time passes of us huddling close, Dad breaks away first, then Mom, wiping her eyes.

"We love you too," Mom answers, Dad nodding behind her, so genuine with admiration on his face.

"Are you okay?" he asks.

Okay is such an ordinary word in a moment when I feel like the heavens should open up with answers, but instead I'm left with more questions. But I won't cry anymore. I won't do it.

Not while I have two people who raised me as their own, loved me more than my real parents could have.

"I think we need to go watch a funny movie and eat ice cream," I suggest, to which Mom laughs.

"Sounds perfect."

With hands on my shoulder, Dad guides me out of the room. "Thank you," he whispers. "You're Mom has cried so much in preparation for this day."

My next breath doesn't come any easier, and I tell myself I have time to dig into my past, see what else I find out about exactly who I am, but for this weekend, I plan to just enjoy my parents' company and pretend everything is normal for all our sanity.

CHAPTER 6

$\mathcal{B}$y the time I arrive back at Raven Academy, it's Monday morning and I'm rushing to my first class. I loved seeing my parents, but my eyes still feel heavy and raw as sleep struggles to come. I haven't been able to stop thinking about how they found me as a baby left on their doorstep. Who does that to a child?

Since finding out, it feels like an invisible vice is squeezing my heart, but I need a distraction before I over-obsess as I have been doing all weekend. I never said another word about this to my parents, not wanting them to worry. Except I'm not fine. I have so many questions about who exactly I am and who my real parents are. Part of me can't help but think the answer is linked to the whole angel confusion, and it hurts my head each time I try to make sense of it.

I step into class ready to lose myself in my studies, and the first lesson passes in a blur, bringing with it a strange comfort in the familiar routine. My next period is free, so I make my way to the library for quiet study time.

The lush lawn outside is long enough that the blades scrape my ankles. Guess the gardener has been slacking off.

"Adeline," Connor calls me from behind, and I groan. "Wait up."

When I turn around, he's running up toward me, and for want of something to say, I nod and pause.

When he gets closer, my breaths speed up, like they always do in his company. Must be a kick-back reaction from the days when I'd swoon in his presence. Even now, he's captivating, but we have too much unresolved past for me to ignore how we left things.

"Been meaning to talk to you but didn't see you around all weekend," he says.

"I spent it at home with my parents. It was kind of nice to get away a bit."

His eyes light up. "How's your dad?"

Thinking of him brings a smile to my face, how happy he was, the good news that he's recovering so fast. "He's doing amazing and he'll probably get the all clear very soon."

"Wow, that's incredible, Adeline. That's a miracle in fact, and I can't tell you how glad that makes me." Instinctually, he reaches over, stroking my arm, his touch sending warmth through me. I still remember how much I'd crave his touch when I crushed on him so hard, I forgot how to breathe. Now, I'm left feeling hurt.

"Come with me," he says, leaning closer. "There are too many eyes out here."

Next thing I know, I'm being tugged along the grounds with him, his grip strong on my arm. But I don't want to go anywhere with him, and I pull free.

"No," I murmur. "Please, Connor, just leave me alone."

But he isn't taking no for an answer and stares at me with persistence in his gaze, like somehow, I belong to him. Like he's allowed to do as he likes. There's so much I want to say to him about our past to make him understand why I'm angry at him. But the crunch of grass coming up behind me steals that opportunity.

"You heard her," Finn's voice carves through the air. "You can leave now, Connor."

Finn stands near me, towering like a warrior come to protect me. His staring match with Connor thickens the air, and neither is

61

backing down. I don't ever remember Connor being this strong, this territorial in his actions before.

"Connor, just go, please," I finally say, well aware Finn will leap into a fight if Connor makes the wrong move. And I don't want anyone fighting over me, don't want Connor hurt even if he deserves it. Every nerve ending in my body is on edge.

Finn takes my hand, laying his claim and I watch as Connor's jawline clenches.

"Remember what I told you, Adeline," Connor states. "Be careful." Then his fiery gaze shoots to Finn, who simply keeps holding my hand, his thumb rubs over my knuckles, soft and gentle as if he's trying to keep me calm.

Connor doesn't say another word but turns and walks away, strolling casually, seemingly unbothered by our confrontation.

Finn's frown turns into a smile when he looks over at me, his expression mesmerizing. My hand is still imprisoned in his, and it feels incredible to have him holding me so protectively.

"Are you okay?" he asks, those captivating eyes filling with sympathy.

I nod. "He didn't hurt me," I admit. "He keeps wanting to talk to me, and I'm not sure I feel ready to talk to him yet."

There's a pause before he speaks, long enough for me to notice and know he's evaluating what I said.

"I'm here if you want to talk about anything, Adi. I'm a fantastic listener. Plus, I've been thinking about you all weekend, waiting for your return, and I'm not ready to let you go just yet." His grin is charming, and sparks of delight race up my spine at his words.

"Feel like going for a walk?" I suggest, suddenly not wanting to be alone either.

He answers only with a grin and his fingers intertwine with mine, awakening the butterflies in my stomach that seem to be ever present nowadays. Finn's personality is like a balm to my nerves and I know that today has changed for the better now that he's with me.

We stroll hand in hand on the outskirts of the school grounds, following the line of woods surrounding the place.

"I don't even know why he came to Raven Academy," I say.

"So, he did something to upset you back at your old school?" Finn asks.

I kick tufts of grass in my path and look up at him. "Feels weird talking to you about him. But he did hurt me really bad, that's all."

"Did he lay a hand on you?" Finn's voice darkens, his grip squeezing lightly.

I shake my head. "No, but he didn't stop the ones who did, and overnight he decided I no longer existed."

"Always knew he was an asshole. He has that asshole face."

"Well, that's the thing," I drag Finn back into our walk after we'd paused. "He's actually kind hearted and was there for me when my dad got cancer, but I just don't understand why he turned into Dr. Jekyll and Mr. Hyde in the end."

"It's clear he likes you," Finn admits. "And he hasn't gotten over you."

I go stiff, my head's fuzzy about having my boyfriend telling me another guy likes me.

Finn's grin morphs into a laugh. "You should see your face. I'm not blind and see lots of guys at school checking you out, so of course Connor wants you back if he lost you. He realizes his mistake."

"This feels awkward talking about this with you," I tell him again. This is Mercy territory, except I'm alone here. Just me and my guys, and something about Finn's calm demeanor always leaves me feeling at ease around him.

"And I can relate," he admits.

I look up at him incredulously then trip over a pothole in the ground, but he catches my elbow and steadies me.

"You had bullies? Impossible."

With a nod, he continues, "When I was younger, my best friend caught me stealing his lunch money, and instead of just shoving me, he ganged up with a bunch of others and shoved me off a steep hill behind the school."

"Ouch! How much money did you take?"

"Three dollars and forty-five cents."

I eye him suspiciously. "How old were you?"

"Ten."

I roll my eyes and shove my hand into his arms. "You were babies."

He chuckles and grabs me back into his arms, embracing me as he moves us forward in an awkward walk. "Well, he still bullied me, and he goes to Raven Academy too."

I dig my heels into the ground and spin around in his arms. "He does? Who is it?"

"Alexander," he says with a smirk.

This time I explode into laughter. "Clearly you two made up."

We are strolling past the woods with a light breeze in our hair, and Finn's company is always calming. I make a note to do this more often and get outdoors a lot more frequent.

"Do you ever get tired of the trees and this weather? All the fog that never seems to go away. I miss the beach and the palm trees sometimes."

"Where is this coming from?" His eyebrows rise.

"Being home with my parents reminds me of things we did together. I don't know, maybe I'm feeling a bit nostalgic I guess, but I remember this amazing trip we took to the Florida beaches one year and something about the place made me fall in love with it. I guess I'm a sucker for a good sunrise."

"It was all those alligators, wasn't it?" he jokes, and I nudge him with my shoulder.

"It was everything, the warm weather, the sound of the waves...I don't know. It's just a place that always brings me joy when I think of it and reminds me of my parents. Maybe one day I'd like to live there."

He takes my arm and brings me to face him. His hands are cupping my face, and he's not saying a word but staring at me with those incredible green eyes. The wind blows his blond hair from his face, and I'm captivated by his beauty. How can he look so divine, leaving me wondering if I'm dreaming that a guy like him would be with someone like me. Just an ordinary girl...well, maybe an ordinary angel. If that's a thing.

"I'll take you to the beaches someday, pretty girl."

His fingers are swirling over my knuckles again sending another wave of excited shivers over me. When he stares at me with such intensity, it feels like someone has sucked all the air from my lungs. He leans in closer, ducking his head to reach me and steal a kiss.

Finn's hands cup my ass and he swings me around, then walks me backward into the woods, away from prying eyes. My back meets a tree, and there he pins me with his body. I cradle myself closer to him, my hands bracing the back of his neck. I stare into eyes brimming with desire.

The bulge in his pants is hard and pressing against my lower stomach.

His fingers skate up my body. "I'm never going to hurt you," he says and takes my lips again. He kisses me softly and passionately, and I barely hold back the burning arousal awakening inside me. I want to wrap my legs around him, so I draw him closer, kissing him with hunger.

He drags his lips over my chin and neck, before taking my earlobe into his mouth. Suckling me gently there, his hands are ravenous beasts, pulling my shirt out of my skirt and snaking up and over my bra.

I moan my pleasure.

He tugs the fabric down, and his fingers are on my hardened nipple.

"Keep doing that," I beg breathlessly.

"You're so fucking hot!" he whispers in my ear. "And I bet you're wet too, baby."

"Holy shit!" My voice comes out hushed as he squeezes my nipple hard, and I tilt my head back against the tree, dying from lust and heat.

Just then the bell rings and Finn takes a step away from me, a huge smirk on his face.

"Nooo," I practically screech, my body on the cusp of release. I just need a few more minutes with his hands...

"Come on pretty girl," he says, laughter threaded through his voice.

"We've got to get you to class. Wouldn't want to mess with your academics for an orgasm."

"I'm okay with messing with them," I tell him emphatically. But he's walking backwards away from me, holding out his hand for me to take so we can head back to the school grounds. I fix my disheveled clothes reluctantly.

"The anticipation will only make everything better," he says with a wink when I walk towards him and take his hand with a groan.

Payback's a bitch, Finn, I think with a small smile as I try to settle myself down. School is going to be torturous for the rest of the day.

CHAPTER 7

The lunch bells rings and I file out of algebra with everyone else. In the hallway, I spot Alexander leaning against the wall, one leg bent and propped up behind him, his arms folded over his chest. He's waiting for me.

I lose my breath at seeing him. He's absolutely captivating. Dark hair swept off his face, his gaze lingering on students passing him, his white school shirt gapes open at his throat. I'm still revved up from Finn's teasing earlier and seeing how sexy Alexander looks only makes it worse.

When our gazes meet, he offers me the most delicious grin and pushes off the wall, then makes his way through the crowd and toward me with the sexiest stroll. He's all shoulders and all I want is to fall against that broad chest.

He collects me into his arms, and the heat on my skin from our touch is electric. It's so alluring, I slip up against him, pressing my chest against his, desperate for him. I don't know what's come over me but being away from Alexander for two days makes me crave him like we've been apart for weeks.

"I missed you so much," he whispers and walks me away from the chaos of the main hall and to a side corridor.

"I couldn't stop thinking about you," I admit, staring at his gorgeous face.

He leans in closer and gently kisses me on my neck, and a moan slips from my lips. His next words come closer to my ear, his hand threading through my hair.

A shiver of excitement rolls through me.

"I had a dream about us last night." He runs his hands down my body.

My heart won't stop racing, and I'm breathing heavily. "Tell me more." I close my eyes, trembling with a crazy passion claiming me, not even minding that we're doing this in the hallway.

"I'd rather show you," he insists, a smile working across his angular face which has the same effect on me as his hands that are sliding lower on my back.

Under his gaze, I'll do anything he asks to taste those lips again.

I lift myself on my toes. "Then show me. I want you. I want us," I whisper in Alexander's ear seductively, then pull back and watch how his controlled demeanor shifts in seconds to one of desire and reck-lessness. I have no idea where my bravery comes from, but in his pres-ence, I can't think of anything else but us together. Not to mention my insides are on fire from this little foreplay.

"No idea where that came from," he admits but takes my hand. "You can have anything and everything you want though, Adi. If that's me, I'm yours."

I laugh as we move fast through the hall and over the school grounds, and I'm buzzing all over at the excitement in his voice, at my own bravery, at my confession. It isn't long before we are standing in his dorm room with the door locked, and he's watching me.

I wind strands of hair around my finger as I admire Alexander unbuttoning his shirt in slow motion like he's giving me a show, his incredible blue eyes sharpening every time he looks down at me.

"You like to tease," I say, trying my hardest not to blush. All my life, I've followed rules, done the right thing, and avoided breaking the law.

Do the right thing and you'll never find trouble, my principal from my old high school used to say. But right now, as Alexander stares at me with a craving darkening his gaze, with his lips parted like he is barely keeping himself restrained, I want all the trouble in the world if it comes in the form of him.

He saunters toward me, peeling his shirt off, pulling it down his strong arms. I stare at his broad chest, practically drooling over his ripped abs and that delicious V-shape where his pants hang low on his hips. Not a word is spoken, I can't find them as I'm burning up and he hasn't even touched me yet. It's illogical the effect he has on me.

"Are you sure about this, beautiful?" He reaches out and takes my hand, then draws me closer.

My heart does a silly thing and beats completely out of rhythm. "Yes, I've wanted this since I first met you."

He raises one of his eyebrows, looking almost astonished, then he smiles, and my legs are melting under me. "You wanted to sleep with me the first time you saw me on the Academy grounds?"

I shrugged nonchalantly. "Maybe I did." I can't remember back that far to what exactly went through my mind, but it was something about losing myself to the beautiful boy in front of me and falling under his spell.

He pushes the curl of hair around my finger behind my ear, his touch leaving a trail of electricity in its wake. "You're adorable when you blush, and I love the way you react so innocently to my touch."

I want to say something smart back, but I'm drowning under the sexy cadence of his voice, drawn to his lips, imagining them dragging over my skin.

He's pulling my top up and over my head, his fingers wrapped around my back and unclasping my bra before he unzips my skirt. Everything falls down to my feet and I'm left standing in my black underwear in front of him. My skin is on fire, nipples pebbled tight under his roaming gaze. I press myself against him, skin to skin, reaching up to kiss him, my hands braced around his neck. My passion is raw and needy, urging him to claim me, to make me forget everything, to make me his.

In one movement, he reaches down and tears my underwear off

me with a savagery that leaves me breathless. I don't move, I'm frozen with anticipation of what's going to happen next.

Hands are on my hips, fingers digging into flesh, he draws my tongue into his mouth. I moan as the bulge in his pants nestles against my lower stomach. Alexander's going to be just the second guy I've ever slept with, but I feel like I'm addicted to sex already with how much I want him. It feels like I've wanted Alexander like this forever and it kind of feels like a dream that it's actually happening.

He breaks from our kiss, his eyes glazed over like he's lost to it. He's looking at me like he's starving and I'm the only thing that will satisfy him.

I need him to need me like that. Because that's how he makes me feel. It's only fair that we're on an even playing field.

He tosses me playfully onto the bed behind me, and laughter slips from me. While he towers over me, his gaze lingers over my naked body, devouring me without a single touch. His pants are tenting in front of him, but I don't dare move to undress him. I get the impression Alexander likes to be in command, which drives me insane with arousal.

"Widen your legs for me, gorgeous," he asks, his eyes like that of a ravenous wolf, lowering over my breasts, my stomach and to the apex between my thighs as I slide them open.

I'll do anything he asks, surer of myself than I've ever been. He reaches down and touches my heat.

I suck in a sharp breath, my body arching from his fingers rocking against me.

"You're so much more beautiful than I could have imagined," he says, his words deep and raspy.

My response is stuck inside me as I soar from his fingers rubbing over my clit. Breathless, my hips sway back and forth under his deft fingers. Waves of pleasure crash through me, and I grasp the bedsheets, a moan on my lips. I'm growing hotter by the second.

With one hand driving me insane, the other unzipping his pants, he never breaks our stare. He pulls away from me for a heartbeat and then he's standing gloriously naked before me. His cock is hard, the tip dotted with a milky tear. He rips open a condom packet with his teeth, then rolls it over himself with ease. I can't help but wonder how many times he's done that, how many girls he's taken to bed, made to feel incredible. But I drive those thoughts away. They don't belong here, not today.

"If I hurt you, you let me know, okay?" He climbs over me and settles between my thighs, his weight over me. He feels cool to the touch, which is welcoming against my fiery body. "You're so innocent, so divine, in ways that make me want to protect you from the world. You're strong and fiery in ways that make me respect you more than you'll ever know."

His tender words surprise me. He's never been that open about what we have.

"You can't hurt me," I say. "But I know you wouldn't even if you could." I unconditionally trust him, and my heart is beaming at hearing what he thinks of me. "Why do you want me so much?" I ask suddenly, needing to know.

He just looks at me, his hands on either side of my shoulders. His mouth lowers toward my collarbone and then moves to take a pebbled nipple into his mouth.

I groan at the sensation of his tongue flicking my nipple, at me losing myself under him.

"All I can think about right now is taking you before I'll go insane."

His words light me up, and he stares down at me, his blue eyes in chaos. "But you're asking me why?"

"Yes," I breathe the word.

He leans forward, his chest against mine, and his mouth claims mine. Our lips and teeth clash, kissing with urgency. I grasp his powerful arms and widen myself for him as he settles between my thighs comfortably, the tip of his hardness pressed against me.

"You make me forget myself, make me feel more alive than I've felt in a long time. You remind me that there is still beauty in this world and it's worth fighting for. When I'm with you I don't need anything else," he admits as if he's confessing a grave sin before my holy altar.

"I feel the same way," I admit.

He brings his lips to mine and his tongue delves into my mouth as he pushes into me. He thrusts in and out of me, groaning against me, stretching me. I dig fingernails into his arms as he takes me. He's buried deep inside, and I'm getting hotter, breaths racing, and nearing the edge of climax so fast with each delicious slapping sound.

Unlike Braxton, Alexander fucks me ruthlessly and deep, laying on top of me like a warrior claiming his prize. His mouth moves over to my neck, teeth grazing over my flesh as he slams into me.

My head tips back, my hands fisting the bed sheets as he rides me.

I can't get enough. I writhe with pleasure; I moan for more.

Alexander is mine. I need him.

Want him.

Desire him.

Miss him.

Adore him.

And I know what my heart wants.

The climax rips through me and I'm exploding. Suddenly, I'm soaring into the sky on Alexander's touch.

I'm shuddering, screaming, and I shut my eyes tight as I glide with ecstasy. I'm completely lost under him. I throw my head back, my body arching off the mattress.

Alexander stiffens over me, roaring at his own orgasm, and I feel him pulsing inside me.

The world around me dissolves behind the pleasure rocking through me. My eyes slip open and he looks at me with such depth in his eyes as if I can look straight into his soul.

"I don't want to lose you," he says with such sincerity that I believe him. He wants me as much as I do him, and I'm scared that if he goes, I'll be a complete mess.

"Then make sure you don't," I say. If I thought my heart was in danger before when it came to the guys in my life, but I'm in real trouble now because I'm all in and they hold the power to completely destroy me if this doesn't work out.

CHAPTER 8

(DANTE)

I'm sitting in the library when I get a text from my father. We haven't spoken since our last fight when he once again threw Alexander in my face about how much I don't measure up to him. It made for a great holiday at home.

I'm sorry.

I look at the text in disbelief. I don't think that my father has ever apologized to anyone in his life, let alone me. But the words are sitting there on the screen in front of me. I'm not sure what to type back. But he texts me again before I can think of anything.

I would like for us to get closer. I've made a lot of mistakes with you, and I have a lot to make up for. Can we talk about everything tonight over dinner?

Now I'm convinced that someone has stolen his phone. Either that or he's been possessed. There's no way that he would say something like this otherwise.

Father?

I type back, still confused. My phone starts to ring as he tries to call me just then, and I drop my phone in surprise. Knowing that I need to prepare myself if I actually am going to have dinner with him, I quickly text him.

I'm fine with dinner.

I'll pick you up around six?

Now I know that he's been possessed. Along with never apologizing for anything, I can't think of any time that he's asked me rather than ordered me to do something.

I'm nervous as I get ready, making sure that I look presentable enough to meet my father's usual expectations. He's always preached that we have a certain image to maintain and I've spent most of my teenage years dressed in pressed pants and blazers much to my displeasure.

I don't know why I'm bothering to get my hopes up. I've been nothing but a disappointment to my father my entire life, this is not going to change now, I think to myself.

But the little boy who's always wanted his father's approval, that part of me, well he's at least a little bit interested in what his father has to say.

My father picks me up in his usual town car. Our driver, Godfrey, gives me a small smile as he opens the door for me. Father is waiting for me inside and he actually gives me a smile that looks somewhat genuine when he sees me. The only time he ever smiles at me is in public when we are in front of important people, so I look around to see if the principal has somehow popped up behind me or some other important member of the Council.

But there's no one there.

It seems he's actually smiling at me.

"It's good to see you, son," he tells me, patting me on the back. I just stare at him blankly, still not sure how I'm supposed to react to all of this. He folds his hands in his lap almost nervously before beginning to speak as we drive off.

"Look Dante," he begins, clearing his throat briefly. "I know we've had our differences over the past few years…"

I cock my eyebrow at him. I would hardly call our issues simply "differences". Maybe mutual hatred would be a better term for our relationship.

He notices my look and clears his throat again. "I've been a terrible man and I've failed you as a father," he says.

My mouth drops open. I've literally dreamt of having a conversation like this with my father for years. Imagined what it would be like for him to actually apologize to me for everything that he's done.

But I don't trust it.

I can't think of any reason for this about face from a man who has continually shown me an amount of disdain normally reserved for your worst enemy, not your son.

"I've come to a realization since our last fight about what I've done. And I want to make this right. I know it will take time, Dante. But I'm willing to put in the work. Will you give me a chance?" he practically pleads with me in an earnest voice.

Now it's my turn to clear my throat. I'm experiencing an inconvenient amount of emotion at my father's words.

"I... would like that," I finally tell him. Because what can I say? Sorry dad, I'm going to hate you forever?

We get to the restaurant. Father has of course picked the fanciest one that the town nearest to the school has to offer. The town actually has quite a few nice offerings due to its proximity to the school and all the wealthy inhabitants of the school and their families. I still prefer the greasy diner that I've been going to the last couple years over anything here though. Thinking about the diner puts a small smile on my face as I think about my date there with Adeline. I wonder what she would tell me to do now in this situation. She would probably tell me to forgive him with everything that's going on with her own father. She's a much better person than I am.

We walk inside and are quickly seated. My father doesn't even leer at our attractive waitress making it an even stranger evening.

"Tell me all about school," he asks after we are settled in our seats and have ordered drinks and some appetizers.

"It's been fine," I tell him, still feeling strange about having a conversation about myself that my father actually seems to be interested in.

He lifts an eyebrow and I'm once again reminded how much I look like him and how much my mannerisms are similar to the man I've despised for so many years. "How has it really been going?" he prods me. And again, the way he's asking makes it seem like he actually wants to know.

So of course, being the lonely boy that I am, desperate for my father's attention even after all these years, I proceed to tell him about my classes, gossip about the various students from families he would be interested in, and what activities I've been engaging in this year. He looks surprised with how well I've been doing in combat training, and it's just a reminder of how little he knows about me.

"And how are your friends?" he asks. I stiffen at the question because Alexander's part of all of that. If I'm real with myself, I would acknowledge that my hard feelings against Alexander are largely the fault of my father.

I put aside my sudden introspection and tell him a little bit about the last party that Nyx through, and Alexander's work with the Council lately, and the artwork that Finn has been working on. My father listens to me like it's the most interesting thing he's ever heard. We pass the rest of dinner in what practically amounts to companionable discussion. He tells me about his work prospects and plans for trips he wants us to go on. It almost feels like when I was younger, and my mom was still alive. My father was a different man back then. Or at least he hid who he really was much better.

It's only when we get back to the car that my father's carefully crafted veneer breaks. "So, any girls at the school catch your attention?" he asked in a voice that sounds intentionally nonchalant.

My skin prickles at the question. I open my mouth to tell him about Adeline, and then stop, something warning me that my dad has ulterior motives with this question.

"You know me, always playing the field," I joke even though the words taste sour in my mouth.

He looks disappointed at my statement, and I get even more suspicious. "Your stepmom was mentioning that you boys have a new classmate this year. I think she said her name was Adeline Jones. She told me Alexander was telling her that she was quite the looker."

I scoff internally. I highly doubt that Alexander would ever tell his mother a girl was hot, let alone ever talk about Adeline with her. My stepmother is a treacherous viper and even Alexander acknowledges that.

"I've seen her around," I say, being intentionally vague.

"Good, good," he says, almost distractedly as if he's thinking hard about something.

"Have you talked to her?" he suddenly asks, once again peering at me closely.

I lick my lips, suddenly sensing danger. "Here and there. She's a scholarship student and a human. And you know we don't mix with our food much unless we have to," I tell him with a dry chuckle.

My father seems frustrated by my answers. "You know I think it's good for us to mix with the humans every now and again," he says.

I can't help but look at him incredulously. This is from the man whom my entire life has lectured me continually on the superiority of our family compared to our kind, and especially compared to humans.

"If she's a scholarship student, then I'm sure she gets good grades. We both know that you could use help raising those grades of yours," he says with a chuckle, apparently now trying to convince me of why I should associate with Adeline.

My heart clenches as he confirms that everything this evening has been fake. He makes it so hard to stand him. If he had listened to anything that I'd told him tonight he would know that my grades are in fact excellent, and I'm in the top five of my class. *He probably wouldn't care about that though since Alexander is at the top of the class*, I think to myself bitterly.

I realize that I've missed something that he's said when he smacks the leather seat next to him to get my attention, his friendly façade cracking for a moment. "Are you paying attention to me, son?" he spits out through gritted teeth, trying to sound nice even though I can see the anger lurking beyond his eyes.

"Of course. You want me to start interacting with the humans," I answer him matter-of-factly. It's almost like I can see the steam start to come out of his ears at my response.

"Well, I was mainly talking about Miss Jones. Deirdre had such good things to say about her based on the reports coming from the school."

It's all I can do not to roll my eyes. Like I could see *Deirdre* of all people ever having something good to say about a scholarship student, let alone a human. My father obviously has ulterior motives, but I'm not connecting the dots of why Adeline has suddenly come into his crosshairs.

Unless he knows... No, there's no way that he knows.

Right?

We're almost to the school when I decide to stop playing around. I've had enough.

"Look, let's just cut to the chase. What is this about? I know that you haven't suddenly become interested in helping the new scholarship student...who's also a human, make friends. So why don't you tell me the truth and drop the charade," I snap at him fiercely.

It's almost fascinating to see the mask he's been wearing all evening dissolve before my eyes. There's a calculating look in his eyes, and his mouth has adopted that smug, arrogant smirk than I'm used to seeing on his face.

It's one that I've spent countless hours daydreaming about knocking off his face.

"Maybe I underestimate you sometimes, son," he sneers. "Okay, let's talk about it. Everyone's buzzing that the new girl at your school is actually an angel. Something that hasn't been seen for hundreds of years if not thousands. Whoever was in possession of her would immediately gain more power than they could ever dream of. That girl is going to be mine."

It's all I can do to keep my face blank. I can feel my hands slightly trembling at his words. This is far worse than anything we thought. My mind begins to race, wondering how in the world we're going to be able to keep her safe, and I'm only half listening to my father.

Do you understand?" he suddenly asks. I try to quickly recall what he was just saying, but I must take too long to answer because there's suddenly a fist flying at my face. I don't react quick enough to move out of the way and he strikes me on my left cheekbone, hitting me so hard that it probably would've collapsed a human skull. As it is, I'll probably sport a bruise for the rest of the day, even with my exhilarated healing powers.

"You're going to make that little bitch think you've fallen in love with her," he hisses at me. "It won't be hard. Documents I've seen on her show that she's been bullied for the past several years. She's probably desperate for attention. Show her a little bit of affection and she'll be eating out of your hand," he orders me, the greed practically oozing out of his eyes.

I know I need to put on the act of my life right now if I'm going to protect Adeline. I school my face into the disdainful, mocking look that I've seen on his face many a time. "You can't be serious. Now I know that you're starting to lose your mind, old man. An angel? You haven't met Adeline Jones, have you? There are more interesting rocks to talk to than her. The only angelic thing she possesses is that fucking, tight body that makes the human males froth at the mouth and follow her like she's in heat. Your sources are wrong, I'm sorry to say. Alexander can tell you that much."

I had barely finished when he's on me, gripping my collar with both hands and shaking me so hard that my neck snaps back.

"Listen you little asshole," he snarls. "You're going to do what I tell you on this. I don't care what she looks like, what she's like, if she's dating someone else... You are going to win her over. If she doesn't do it willingly, you will force her to come to me. There're too many eyes on her right now, we can't make any moves until Christmas break when we can get her off campus on the premise that she's going to visit her parents. You have until then to get it done. You will not fail me on this." He seems desperate, as if his very life depends on Adeline.

"Why do you need her so bad? What if you're wrong...which you are. And you end up kidnapping a human whose disappearance will actually matter," I tell him, keeping that same disdained tone in my voice.

His face shifts for a second and I can see the fear that my words evoke that he could be wrong. The fearful look is gone when I blink.

"I'm willing to take that chance," he says coldly as we pull up to the front of Raven Academy. "You have until Christmas break, Dante," he reinforces again as he finally lets go of my shirt collar. He pulls out his cell phone, furiously typing on it as he ignores my presence.

Seething anger hits me so hot and thick that it's hard to see past my rage. The monster inside of me is itching to come out and attack him. Only the worry about what would happen to Adeline if he ended me in a fight right now keeps me at bay.

I leave the car without another word to him. I obviously need to start looking into what my father's been up to. I understand the lure an angel has from a feeding perspective, but the desperation that I just saw from him was more than just that.

Anxiety threads through my gut. We're operating in all unknowns right now. Sure, we know that Adeline is an angel, but we still have very little knowledge of what that means as far as her abilities, the danger she's in, anything really...And now I have to worry about my father's intentions as well. Panic joins my anxiety.

Adeline.

I have to tell her what happened tonight. I don't want her to ever doubt my intentions. I know that Braxton and Alexander still don't trust me, and I can live with that. What I can't live with is Adeline thinking that I want her for the wrong reasons.

I should probably go immediately to gather the guys to talk about what just happened. But I just want to see her. Beyond the shitshow that just happened, disappointment is still curling in my insides about how he had acted at the start of tonight. It had been my wishes coming true at least for a few hours.

I was such a fucking fool.

I realize that it's after midnight as I stand in front of her door, and I'm oddly nervous all of a sudden. It also strikes me that one of the other guys could be with her right now. Is it even worth knocking if she has one of them in her bed?

Yes, I decide. For this clusterfuck to work we will all have some moments when one of us will need her at an inconvenient time to one of the others. Right now, I need her, and the rest of them will just have to deal with it.

The door opens before I can even knock and Adeline is standing there, looking like an ethereal princess in a gauzy nightgown.

"Dante?" she asks sleepily. Looking beyond her into her darkened room, I'm relieved to see that her bed is empty. I know that one of the guys will be nearby standing guard to her room as we've been doing every night, but at least I'll be the only one in her bed.

That is, if she even wants me in there after I tell her about the fact that my family is one of her hunters.

"Dante, what happened to you?" she practically screeches suddenly, looking much more awake than she had been a second ago. She reaches out a hand to gently brush my face and I'm reminded of how bad I must look from my dad's hit. I'm tempted to lie to her for a second and say that I got it in gym or something like that, old habits die hard after all, but I choke the truth out. I don't want to lie to her. I just want to love her.

"Had dinner with my father tonight. It didn't go great."

She takes my hand and leads me inside her room, shutting the door closed behind her. It smells like her, a mixture of vanilla and honey, the result of her favorite lotion at the moment, and I breathe in the scent, letting it relax me.

She leads me by the hand to her bed and gently has me sit down. She touches my face, tracing the injury lovingly. I lean into her hand, closing my eyes as I soak up her touch. I pull her wrist briefly from my face and kiss it softly.

After a moment she pulls away from me and walks to the small mini fridge she keeps drinks in and pulls out a cold can of Diet Dr. Pepper. She walks back towards me and holds it against my face as a makeshift ice pack.

"What happened tonight?" she says softly, stroking my hair with her other hand.

I laugh bitterly. "It was a shit show, how every second I spend with my father is," I contemplate not telling her about everything that happened, but there's a part of me that wants her to know. Can she handle the worst part of me and still want me? There's only one way to find out.

"We've talked about this, but my father and I have had a terrible relationship for a very long time. The last time I was home...it didn't go very well. We had a huge fight that ended with a brawl basically. He did his usual thing where he threw Alexander in my face and I just snapped. We hadn't spoken since then. He texted me out of the blue today and apologized..." I pause, feeling ridiculously choked up rehashing it.

"There was a little bit today when I actually thought that things were going to be different, that somehow he had softened towards me. That we might actually have a relationship." I looked at her brokenly. "Isn't that the most ridiculous thing you've ever heard? What kind of idiot am I that I would forget years and years of total bullshit at a couple of nice lines from him?"

"The kind of idiot that just wants to be loved by his father," she says gently. "Anyone would want that."

"I'm weak," I choke out. "Just like he always tells me I am."

"I think being able to forgive and love takes a lot more strength than hate does," she tells me, surprising me with a soft kiss on my lips. A rush of warmth filters through my senses. Closing my eyes, I savor the sweetness of her lips while my heart beats rapidly, an effect she's had on me from the very beginning.

"So how did tonight end with your face looking like that if it started with him apologizing," she asks.

I'm silent as I prepare myself for her reaction to my dad's plan. "He knows you're an angel somehow," I tell her softly. "He was trying to butter me up so that I would try to get close to you in order for him to use you." I'm braced for her disappointment, not able to look at her face, so it's a shock to me when she tilts my head to look at her. There's so much love pouring out of her that I can barely believe it.

"You were afraid to tell me that, weren't you?" she guesses. I just nod. "Dante, you aren't responsible for your father's actions, just like Alexander isn't responsible for your father's actions."

"You aren't worried at all that I'm just trying to get close to you to help out my father?" I ask her incredulously. "How could you even trust any of us after everything we put you through when you first arrived."

She laughs. "Maybe I'm a fool, but I feel like I know your heart. And it would never betray me."

A sound that's a mixture of a sob and a laugh bursts out of my mouth as I bury my head against her neck, breathing in her perfect scent. "I think you're the first person in my life besides my mother to ever believe in me," I mutter against her neck. "Why does family have to be so hard?"

"There's the family that we're born with and the family that we choose. But I think the family we choose will always be better at knowing our hearts," she answers as she softly strokes my hair.

"I choose you, Adeline. I'll choose you every time. Until the end of time I'll choose you," I tell her, the promise burning into my heart, never to be broken.

"I choose you too, Dante. Always," she whispers to me.

And in that moment, I know that I don't need my father...I don't need anyone but her. I'll always have a home. It will be wherever she is.

I pull her to me urgently, pressing my lips against hers like I need her touch to survive.

Fuck.

Every kiss I've ever had before this one is a hollow, false version of what a kiss should be like. Nothing compares. I crave her. The passion between us spikes higher and higher. I have no control of the flames overcoming me. It takes everything in me to gently, but insistently break our kiss. My first time making love to her isn't going to after I've spent the evening with my father.

"Why?" she asks in a raspy, out of breath voice.

"We'll have our perfect moment, and when I'm sporting the black eye that he gave me isn't it," I explain, and she ruefully nods.

"I'm falling in love with you, Dante," she whispers softly.

"I've already fallen," I respond.

There's nothing I won't do for this girl. Nothing.

CHAPTER 9

(ADELINE)

"Your assignment is due next week. Two-thousand-word essay," Mr. Dusk announces to the class who respond in groans. "Gargoyle architecture was meant to scare away evil spirits, but where did the concept of such statues coming to life come from?"

I frantically make notes, already planning out the essay in my head, and I've decided to head to the library during a free period I have coming up for research.

Mr. Dusk breaks into a discussion about where the first gargoyle is recorded on buildings. Egypt, Greece, and China have the earliest versions, but the gothic ones I've seen commonly in movies comes from Europe.

I take more notes, but my mind keeps returning to Alexander and Dante, to memories I will never forget. My stomach is tingling with the reminder of how my body hummed beneath Alexander. The way he made love to me was primal and filled with hunger, but the tenderness in his eyes had me melting. His words still linger in my mind. He opened up, showed me a part of himself that touched me, left me desiring him endlessly. My face warms at the memory of what he did to my body, and small jolts of the euphoria I experienced the night before zip to the pits of my stomach. I also can't get Dante out of my head. It felt like we took a huge step in our relationship last night. I'll never forget him telling me that he was choosing me. I choose him too.

I lift my gaze to Mr. Dusk still waffling on, noting Clarissa sitting in the front row, eyeing him while her hand grazes over her breast, catching his attention. He stumbles over his words, and I roll my eyes that she harasses me while she's having an affair with a teacher too and flirting with him in plain sight of everyone.

Hypocrite.

As she shifts in her seat, I see she's wearing a mini school skirt, her legs not exactly closed, and she's got on white gold hoop earrings and a matching delicate bracelet. Did Mr. Dusk gift them to her? They look expensive. I still don't understand why she hates me so much because to me it seems she has everything she wants.

When class ends, I notice she lingers behind, so I quickly scoop up my books and rush out of the class, making my way to my locker to dump them.

My stomach is growling, the hunger deepening. After a quick detour into the food hall where I eat a chicken salad sandwich in record time, I sneak out an apple and make my way to the library, biting into the crisp, green fruit as I walk.

A buzz vibrates in my pocket and I pull out my phone and see a message from Mercy. I smile instantly and tap it open.

Hope you're not getting up to anything perverted with the hot squad while I'm not there. Miss you so much.

If only she knew the half of it, and I frantically type my response as I stroll over the lawn.

Me! Yep, I'm an utter angel. But as I hit the send button, I stare at the last word and swallow hard. I wish I could speak to her freely, tell her what others seem to believe after my blood test and have her help me make sense of it all. Though knowing Mercy, she'll believe it in a heartbeat and find some evidence online on her conspiracy websites confirming angels are living amongst us.

The phone beeps and I glance down at her message.

Starting a new school next week. Shitting bricks. Wish you were with me.

Me too, I type back, wanting to tell her about my time with Alexander. I say nothing and instead write; *Clarissa is being a major bitch face.*

Slap her hard, and she'll back off. LOL

I laugh at her response and push past the glass door of the library; the stale smell of books is barely masked by the vanilla air freshener scent lingering in the air. Tucking the phone into my back pocket, I toss the apple core into a bin and walk toward the computers.

After a quick search on the digital catalogues for gargoyles, I make my way up to the first floor and walk down an aisle flanked by rows and rows of books. There's always something comforting about being surrounded by so much knowledge right at my fingertips. So much exists online, but nothing will replace the feeling of holding a book, the paper between my fingers, the captivating smell. Plus, essays always ask for references, and I know Mr. Dusk frowns down upon online references.

Running a finger over the spines, I pull out a book titled, *Modern Mythologies,* and I scan the index for gargoyles, flicking to the page and scanning the text after I find it.

A hand gingerly touches my shoulder, and I whip around in surprise, the book dropping from my grasp and hitting the floorboards with an echoing thud.

Connor stands in front of me, smirking, and in that sliver of a second, the light from the window behind me hits him in an angle that has my heart beating faster. I'm seeing him like we're in our old school where that smile of his used to lift the heaviest troubles off my shoulders. Where my knees would go weak in his presence. Where I craved nothing else but for him to want me as much as I did him.

"Never seen you in the library before. You're either hiding from someone or you genuinely haven't entered the digital age of information."

Reality settles in at his statement reminding me of who he really is and his betrayal, and all I can think about now is wanting to smack the smirk off his face.

I sigh and roll my eyes. "Is that why you're here? Hiding from someone? You have a tendency to get on people's nerves, so it wouldn't surprise me." I can't believe I once liked him and wanted to date him. He's beyond handsome, I'll give him that. He's strong and muscular and I've seen girls drool over him. Even the way he looks at me now, his gaze dipping over me stirs something in my gut. It shouldn't and it annoys me that I react with anything but anger toward him. I'm obviously some kind of masochist.

He doesn't respond right away, but pins me with his stare, clearly not expecting me to quip back at him.

"I followed you here," he says, his voice darkening.

"Wow, that's a super creepy thing to do and admit."

He shrugs, completely not put off by my comment or how stalk-erish he sounds. "It's the only way to get you alone without one of your boyfriends lurking nearby."

I lift a brow, remembering Clarissa's words about how many guys I want in my harem, about the school talking about me. My heart starts beating faster, hating how quickly everyone judges.

"What do you care who I'm with? Actually, forget it, *I* don't care." As I turn away from him, I remember he stopped Dixon from raping me, and he might know more about what's going on at this school. With that comes guilt that I snapped at him. *Damn! Great work, Adi!*

Taking a deep breath, I turn towards him with a smile. "Look, sorry, I'm just a bit jumpy right now. I meant to thank you for stopping Dixon the other day. What you did--"

"I'd do it again and again in a heartbeat. That son of a bitch deserved everything he got." There's a sincerity behind his words, and something I can completely respect and connect with.

When I look at him, I see the guy from my old school, the one who was kind to me for a while. Who comforted me when my dad fell sick, who made me believe he was a friend and maybe so much more. Until he stopped talking to me or pretending I existed because his ex, Alexia caught us at a cafe. He broke me that day.

Words teeter on the edge of my mind, but they won't come. Words I've carried with me ever since Connor shattered me. And even now after this long, I can't bring myself to say them.

His gaze flickers to my lips, and my heart beats faster under his gaze. The corner of his mouth twitches like he might break out into a smile. He's so much stronger now, his muscles more defined, his face as handsome as always. I curse myself in my head that I allow myself to even contemplate such things.

"I better go." I bend down to pick up the dropped book, laying open on a page about Dracula's myth starting in Romania, and the word *devil* catches my attention. I scan the line quickly about the Romanian word, Dracul meaning devil and it's how the word Dracula came about. The whole myth is based on a Wallachia prince who viciously staked his enemies and gained himself the nicknames, Vlad Dracul or Vlad the Dragon. I can't help but think of the enormous stone dragon wrapped around the main building on the Academy grounds.

I feel Connor's eyes on me, and I stare at his black boots, the tips scuffed and dusty with dirt like he'd been spending a lot of time outside. I stand and push the book back onto the shelf.

"See you," I say and turn to leave.

Connor snatches my wrist and sidles up to me, his fingers feather soft against the tender skin on the inside of my wrist. A zip of electricity jolts up my arm and through my body, the kind that has zero to do with giving me a static shock, but my damn body reacting to things it shouldn't.

"Will you ever forgive me, Adeline?"

My jaw trembles and I go frozen-still. Something about the softness in his voice opens the floodgates in my head. "You hurt me so fucking bad. I thought you liked me, even as a friend, but what you did was an asshole thing. And I know I saw you watching me as Alexia beat me up that day outside the school. Did that do it for you?" I'm shaking all over because I don't want to talk about this at all, let alone in a library where anyone nearby could hear us, but it all comes gushing out regardless.

"Adeline, it's nothing like that," he pleads, the sorrow deepening in my gaze, but I don't believe him. How can I? My head swims, and the memory plays over and over in my head.

Alexia and her gang shoving me to the ground, kicking and punching me. I broke a rib that day from what they did. I met Connor's eyes for a split second from the corner of the school before he vanished and left me with the bitch gang.

I rip my hand from his. "Then what's it like?" I snap.

A shadow shifts two rows away, and I lower my voice. "What possible reason did you have for throwing me to the wolves?"

He rakes a hand through his short black hair, lips pinching tight, and looks at me through his lowering lashes.

"You want to know the truth?"

"Yes, that's why I'm asking."

"I was starting to have such deep feelings for you," he confesses. "It scared me."

My mouth feels like it's been left open for weeks and moths have made a home inside. "What'? Because of Alexia?" I gape.

He's shaking his head. "I never should have dated her in the first place. I'm sorry if I hurt you, and I handled the situation fucking atrociously. I go over that moment every single day, hating myself for not stepping in." He pauses, his gaze lowering like he's picturing it in his mind. "Maybe you'll learn to forgive me one day which is why I'm trying to make it up to you now by keeping you protected." His features morph into sorrow and sympathy.

"I don't know what to say," I explain with no inflection in my voice, standing numb on the spot. For so long I let myself fall for Connor and now to hear he left me because he liked me too leaves me shaking fiercely, a sharp ache settling in my heart. I feel wrecked. "I have to go," I murmur, my mind spinning with information overload.

"Just one more thing," he says, and I stop in my tracks, glancing back over my shoulder. "I need you to open your eyes to what's going on at this school, Adi for your own sake. Have you ever wondered why there are no mirrors anywhere, not even in the bathroom? What do you think you'll see if you look at the other students' reflection?"

He tilts his head back, watching me, expecting a reaction. But I'm drowning in reactions right now, and I want to be alone to sort out my muddled thoughts, the conflicting emotions that Connor always gives me.

Tension pulses through my muscles. "What do you mean?"

Connor groans and turns away from me before heading down the stairs to the lower level without another word. A bang sounds behind me, and I flinch around to find a blond girl has dropped a book out of the pile in her arms. Her friend helps and they giggle as they move to a nearby study table.

What in the world is going on with Connor? And what's the deal with the butterflies that had taken residence in my stomach around him suddenly.

I can't stand being in the library a second longer, so I hurry downstairs and outside.

Why there are no mirrors anywhere.

The more I think about it, the more I can't recall seeing a mirror anywhere in the school. I found it strange on my first day not seeing one in the bathroom, but thought nothing more of it. Every school had unusual rules and I expected some quirkiness in a school as old as Raven Academy. But now, Connor's words drum through my mind.

My walk transforms into a run, and I'm rushing to my room. I burst past the door and storm to my toiletries bag. Rummaging through it, I pull out my small compact mirror. The one I've been using since arriving on campus to get ready. I'm mad with curiosity. Connor knows something but seems insistent on me working it out myself, or maybe he knows I most likely won't believe him. And now I want to know why there aren't mirrors at Raven Academy.

Fingers curling over the compact mirror, I storm back into the hallway, making my way outside, when Liam, the golden-haired boy from my chemistry class passes me. He sneers my way. We're not exactly on friendly terms after our school camping trip.

I head outside where the grounds are empty.

Once he passes me, I lift the mirror and flip it open, then stare into it over my shoulder, finding Liam strolling with his hands in his pockets away from me.

I huff a breath. What was Connor talking about? Or am I doing this wrong?

Inside the main building where the lessons are held, students are everywhere, jostling against me, and I jerk forward when someone accidentally kicks the back of my knee in the crazy stampede of getting to class. I need to do the same, but I need to first find out if there's anything to what Connor says.

So, I push myself into the crowd to where everyone is and turn my back before lifting the mirror. I position it so I'm glancing through it to those standing behind me. I'm sure I'm seeing wrong as there are only maybe half a dozen students showing in the mirror despite the fact that the corridor is cram packed around me. I look back and there are at least three dozen students. My hand tightens on the mirror, and I look again, keeping my eyes trained on the room. In the mirror there are far fewer students then when I look at them with the naked eye.

My head hurts trying to make sense of what I'm seeing.

Someone brutally slams into my shoulder and my hands flinch, the mirror slipping from my grip.

I gasp and dive for it amid the masses, but I can't see it.

Crunch.

The familiar sound of glass shattering reaches me, and I die a little on the inside.

Shit!

"Adi, are you okay?" Dante asks.

I jolt to my feet, blinking hard, trying to see clearly through the fog inside my head.

"You look flushed." He takes my hand in his and guides me away from the horde.

Breath flees my lungs as I scan the ground where the mirror lays trampled and smashed into a thousand pebbled shards. The image of what I saw stays with me, it rolls over me, and I can't understand it.

"You alright?" he asks again.

I nod and look up at him, pushing my lips into a smile. "Yeah, I'm fine," I lie. "Just have a headache."

His hand slides around my waist and confusion flares up inside me. All I can think is I need to find Connor and ask him what in the fucking world does the mirror not reflecting everyone means.

"You want me to take you back to your room?" Dante asks, and I feel horrible for ignoring him.

I lean in closer to him, his male scent invading my nostrils, making my heart pound harder. "I'd like that."

He leans closer and guides me down the hall where the crowd seems to split open for us to pass like Dante somehow holds sway over them.

I slip inside my room once we reach it without him, using my headache as an excuse to reinforce my need to be alone.

Once inside, I lean against my door, my heart beating a thousand beats a minute.

What kind of creature doesn't have a reflection and how the hell did I end up surrounded by all of them at this school?

CHAPTER 10

That night, I can't stop thinking about how I found Alexander and Dante with that girl in their dorm so many weeks ago. After they swore to me that it wasn't what it looked like, we kind of moved on. I never did get any answers. How did that happen? What exactly were they doing? I was usually a smarter girl than that.

It isn't that I don't believe them that nothing happened between them sexually, it's that obviously there is something going on, something that I didn't comprehend back then, even while staring right at the scene. My mind darted to the image of Dixon sucking the white mist out from Mercy's mouth. That weird way that Mercy would act sometimes. Were Dixon or her ex feeding on her somehow? Then there were the missing mirrors, the supernatural strength and speed. The inhumanly good looks. The yearbooks...the weird way that scholarship students acted around here. The list went on and on.

I had been operating with my head in the ground, a part of me most likely not wanting to disrupt this fragile little bubble we had been developing lately where everything was good. Laying in my bed with my tortured thoughts, I realize that none of it has been real. I mean they know I'm an angel, but have they offered up what they are?

No. They haven't. Every time we even get close to the topic, they shut down and I can see the fear lurking in their eyes. Whatever they are, it's going to rock my world. Maybe not as much as finding out that I'm an angel though. It's one thing to find out that someone else is something strange...but finding out you are too, whole different ball game.

It's four am when I can't take it anymore. I have to know what they're hiding. And if they don't tell me, well then, we're done. It's as simple as that.

I throw on a sweatshirt over my thin sleep shirt and open the door, giving a small squeak when I see Finn sitting next to my door, leaning against the wall as he watches YouTube videos.

He looks at me in surprise and quickly stands up. "What's wrong? Why are you up?"

"What are you doing outside of my door?" I retort, irrationally angry.

He looks at me with confusion. "We told you that you weren't ever going to be alone. Someone has been by your door every night since Dixon happened."

"Oh," I say, feeling stupid as I remembered them saying that. "Why haven't you been coming inside then?"

"You haven't invited anyone in even though one of us asks you every night if you want us to stay with you," he replies slowly.

"Right," I say, feeling guilty that I've been forcing them to sit out in the hallway every night when I could have been cuddled up with them in my bed.

But then I remember why I came out here in the first place, and my guilt disappears. As far as I'm concerned, they don't deserve anything from me.

"Adi," Finn says gently, touching the side of my face as he speaks. "What's wrong?"

My lip quivers, a mixture of anger and irrational sadness overwhelming me. "I need you to tell me the truth. I need to know what you are," I tell him in a raspy voice.

He freezes. I can see the alarm flood his features. "I..."

"Don't try and get out of this conversation, Finn," I cut him off sharply. "I will find out the truth tonight or we're done. I'm not above threats on this."

Finn looks devastated. "Adeline, please..."

"Tell me!" I shriek before looking around the hallway quickly to see if anyone is around.

He lets out a frustrated sigh and then seems to come to a decision. He types something furiously into his phone and then grabs my arm and begins to march me down the hallway.

"Where are we going?" I ask, as I jog to keep up with his frantic pace.

"You wanted answers, Adeline, and now you're going to get them," he replies tersely, obviously angry at the situation I'm putting him in.

I personally don't feel bad about it at all.

I'm surprised when he walks me to Braxton's room. Before he can even knock, Braxton is opening the door, a tense look on his face. He opens the door wider and gestures us to come in, still without saying a word.

The rest of the guys are waiting in his apartment, the same tense, almost frightened looks on their faces.

For a second, I'm tempted to let it go, just so I don't have to see them looking like this. I push that thought immediately away. I deserve answers. I need answers.

Braxton closes the door once we're all inside, and then he locks it and leans against it, as if he's blocking the only exit in the room just in case I decide to try and escape after what they tell me.

It only serves to make me more nervous about what I'm going to hear. My mind has been racing all night, trying to think of what they could possibly be. Some kind of witch? A demon? There were so many possibilities. When I tried to Google it, it only made me more confused.

What kind of paranormal creature feeds on a white mist from someone? What in the world is the white mist?

I have so many questions.

The silence is deafening in the room. They're all staring at me, and

I'm not sure what they're waiting for. They know why I'm here. I guess I'm going to have to force out every answer that I want.

"Which one of you is going to tell me what you are? Are you all the same things, or are you different?" I begin, sitting down in one of Braxton's plush armchairs and trying to look relaxed. I can probably get more answers out of them if I look calm, like I'm not going to bolt at any second.

"What do you think we are?" Braxton asks curiously. "Any theories?"

"You told me that day in my room that you weren't an angel. Just by the way that you reacted then, and the way you're reacting now, you must be closer to a demon," I begin slowly. The word 'demon' makes me remember the book I was reading earlier. The one about the demons from Transylvania. The devils.

"What are you thinking right now?" Dante asks.

"Do you feed off of the white mist too?" I blurt out, shivering as I think about what it had looked like. The guys all appear confused.

"White mist?" Dante questions.

"Dixon was feeding off of Mercy when Adeline found them," Braxton explains before I can answer.

"I see," Dante answers.

Braxton takes a deep breath; I look over briefly at Alexander who is unusually quiet. He's just watching me with an unfathomable gaze.

"In answer to your question, we do feed off the white mist. We depend on it to survive," explains Braxton matter-of-factly.

I blanch at the fact that the five guys I'm dating have the same dangerous propensities as Dixon, a creature who's killed other students, who fed off my best friend, and who almost killed me.

"Let's all stop trying to protect Adeline's delicate sensitivities," comments Alexander sarcastically. "Adeline's promised to love everyone in this room at one point or another, hasn't she? That's not going to change because of a little thing like this," he says challengingly, still not taking his eyes off of me as if he's daring me to say differently.

The room's heavy as if everyone is waiting with bated breath for me to answer Alexander's question. When he sees that I'm not going to rise to his question, he goes for it.

"My sweet angel, we're vampires," he says bluntly with a smug smile on his face.

I watch in an awestruck horror as his canine teeth start to lengthen and sharpen right in front of me. "Our kind has hunted your kind, enslaved them, and killed them practically since the beginning of time."

Sick fear curdles in my stomach as his new teeth gleam under the lighting of the room. But I also have a million questions. As far as I know, vampires can't go out in the daylight...and the five of them clearly can. The white mist hardly looked like blood. They aren't really fitting any of the stereotypes that human beings are raised to think about vampires.

Alexander is glaring at me, just daring me to go screaming out of the room. Maybe a rational person would be afraid. And honestly a part of me is terrified.

But I know these men. I've felt what's in their hearts. We're like a twisted version of Romeo and Juliet except Romeo never wanted to eat Juliet.

"It's rather fascinating then with that kind of history between vampires and angels, that the five of you have fallen in love with one, isn't it?" I finally answer after a breath.

It takes a moment, but eventually Nyx starts to chuckle at my response. He's always the one with the best sense of humor, so it isn't a surprise that he would find some kind of joke in this situation. "You've got balls of steel, my love," he comments, eliciting a snort from the others around us and alleviating some of the tension.

My next sentence sobers everyone up though. "I've never seen you drink blood," I say quietly. "So, what do you feed on with *those* things?" I ask, gesturing to Alexander's still extended teeth.

"We drink blood occasionally," admits Finn. "But it's so we can walk in the daylight," he says. "The effects of even drinking a little bit stay with us for quite a while so it's only sometimes. Whoever decided to spread the rumor that we were bloodthirsty obviously didn't know

97

our kind very well. We don't even really like the blood directly from the vein."

"So, what *do* you feed on?" I ask, cringing as the question once again slips out. I somehow know that the truth of what they eat is far worse than blood. The silence in the room after my question feels heavy, filled with expectations and fears.

"We feed off souls," Braxton whispers to me in a gravely, tense voice. "Every hope and dream, every devastation and failure...they all taste differently...and we feed off them all. It's what makes you so valuable to our kind, Adeline. Your soul is so much purer than a humans, it provides us with a high we don't ever come down from. Your soul doesn't break and sliver like a human's when we feed, it stays completely perfect no matter how much is taken from it. One taste of your kind is the equivalent to heroin for our people."

"The white mist was a part of Mercy's soul.... Dixon fed on our souls?" I ask in a panicked whisper. I thought that I had a handle on this paranormal stuff, after all, I didn't think anything would top finding out that I was an angel. But I had been wrong. Finding out that vampires existed, and they not only fed off of blood, but also souls. This was a lot to take.

"Your angelic bloodline was the only thing that saved you after Dixon fed on you that night," Braxton continued in a haunted voice. "Any human who had that much of their soul taken would have been nothing but a shell afterwards."

My mind races as I think about all the strange things at this school, the strange way a lot of the students acted. It was starting to all make sense.

"That's the difference between the scholarship students and the non-scholarship students...isn't it. We're brought here to be your food." I can't hide the heavy dose of disgust present in my voice. "Is everyone lured here with the promise of something they desperately need, like my father's medical bills?"

I feel wounded. I thought that all the misunderstandings between the guys and I had been solved. But this is huge. I was literally brought here to be their food source. I couldn't have even imagined something this insane as the backstory of who the guys really were.

They exchange looks. "We think that one was special for you. Someone must have had suspicions that you were something unique and wanted to make sure you ended up at the school. The rest of the students were just offered scholarships as far as we know," Braxton explains.

I look at Alexander and Dante. "That girl that I found you with... you were feeding off of her, weren't you?" I murmur, feeling sick as I envision the scene that I walked into. The both nod guiltily. "Sometimes we have to use certain "tactics" to get humans where we want them. If they're scared or angry...they won't taste as good. We had just used a bit of compulsion on her to get her relaxed," murmurs Dante tentatively, looking scared that I was going to bite his head off. "But nothing actually happened. There was no kissing or anything," he quickly continues when he sees the furious look on my face.

I decide not to go anymore into that. I don't think I want to hear about their seduction tactics to entice their food. I understand better why they're so beautiful. Aren't the most dangerous predators in nature, usually the most beautiful. Being able to easily lure in your food is necessary.

"You said that feeding on a soul can fracture a human's soul. Does it make them act weird after it? Or are the students at this school really just that strange?"

Finn grimaces at my question, so I turn my attention to him to provide the answer to my question. "There's always a period of adjustment after we feed. There are rules in place of how often we can feed on one person. But...sometimes those rules get broken." He hesitates before continuing averts his eyes from me so that he's looking at the ground instead of my face. "There are certain souls that taste better than others. Happier souls have a different taste than depressed souls. Good people usually taste much better than those with a lot of sin in their history. It's all preference really, but if a student here is known to taste better than others, the rule of limiting feeds ends up getting broken quite a bit."

I think of Jenny and how strange she always seems, like she's constantly on the verge of a mental breakdown. But Mercy also acted that way a lot lately. Was she getting fed on too much? Had the guys...

"Did you feed on Mercy?" I ask in a horrified voice, already knowing what their answer is going to be. Mercy is one of the best people I've ever met. I'm sure her soul tastes like candy, if that's possible for a soul.

They all look guilty and my heart sinks. I'm oddly jealous though as well.

What is wrong with me?

"Have you fed off of her since we started dating?" I ask, in a voice that isn't very good at hiding how upset I am right now.

"It was just me who fed on her once," says Nyx guiltily. "But it hasn't happened since you came to the school. We just would make her go back to her room anytime she was in the way of us getting to you."

Finn shoots him a dirty look before speaking. "We didn't exactly make her off limits to other people though, Adeline. If we're going to be admitting everything tonight, I guess we should admit that Mercy hasn't been very high on our priority list."

"How did you send her away?"

"We can compel other creatures when we need to. The stronger the vampire, the stronger the compulsion. Our compulsion also is affected by how strong or weak the person is. As I'm sure you're aware, Mercy deals with a lot of self-doubt. It makes it easier for us to influence her and others like her. Basically, high school students can all be controlled very easily. They're all a mess."

I'm about to yell at them for compelling Mercy when I realize that I have no memory of them sending Mercy away. "You said you sent Mercy away when you wanted to get close to me," I begin slowly, trying to figure it out. "Where was I when this was happening?"

The guilt in the air ramps up a notch...or two. No one answers. I look at each of them, trying to understand.

Suddenly it hits me. "Have you fed off of me?" I choke out.

Still nobody answers and I'm dying inside. The fuckers actually have. They're just like Dixon. Had I been near death before and just didn't remember it.

"Adeline..." Braxton says brokenly, taking a step towards me.

"Don't come any closer," I hiss out as tears start sliding down my cheeks. Braxton stays still but Alexander is on me before I can say another word, disregarding everything I have to say like usual.

"You aren't allowed to push us away because of this," he says angrily, gripping my chin in his hand fiercely before slamming his lips against mine.

I rip my lips away from him and glare at him. "I can do anything I want," I tell him angrily, pushing him away from me. He takes a few steps back and glares at me.

"You knew we weren't good from the very beginning. We didn't exactly do anything to hide that. We didn't know you when you came here. It wasn't like it is now. You have to differentiate between then and now. We would never feed on you without your permission now. I won't let you turn away from us after how far we've come. You're mine, and that's not going to change even if you're angry. We're never letting you go."

In a fit of rage, I lunge at Alexander, my heart racing, my only intention to get him to shut the hell up through any means necessary. But he's much too quick for me to get a jump on him. In a flash of heat and burning blue eyes and and bared teeth, the bastard's got both of my wrists firmly in his grasp and he's pulling my screeching body back towards him.

In one fluid motion he shoves me back into my chair and leans me backwards, pinning my arms above my head, and pressing himself against me. I can feel the unmistakable sensation of his hard-on pushing against me. I'm not proud of it, but I lose all resolve to resist him, grinding myself against his hardness and straining my face up to kiss him. The second my lips make the barest of contact with his, he groans loudly and presses his lips against mine like a man possessed.

Someone clears their throat loudly just then and I freeze, becoming aware that I was about to let Alexander mount me in the middle of the room. Alexander pulls away from me with a triumphant chuckle and I roll my eyes.

He somehow succeeded in extinguishing my anger. Sexy bastard.

But thinking of what he said, he's right. As long as they haven't fed on me since we became "this" ...whatever "this" is, I can't really blame them. These are not good boys, and combined with the fact that their vampires, it isn't really surprising that they were tempted to try the new girl's soul.

"You promise me you haven't tried my soul lately?" I ask begrudgingly, annoyed with myself for letting this go so easily.

They all immediately begin to assure me they haven't, and I smirk a little bit at how desperate they sound.

I sigh and then continue to pepper questions at them. "Why don't I remember any of this?" I ask, frowning as I struggle to remember being alone with them in the beginning.

"It's part of the feeding and the compulsion," Braxton explains. "It makes you forget so that you won't tell anyone, and we can do it again later."

"Except you have something about you, I guess an angelic trait or something, that makes it very hard for you to be compelled," says Finn, an interested look in his eye.

"What do you mean?"

"Every time we tried to compel you in the beginning you would come out of it quickly. We could still get you to forget things, but we couldn't make you do anything for more than a few minutes."

"How often did you try to make me do things?" I practically screech. Finn holds up his hands in supplication. "Calm down. It was only in the beginning as well," he tells me soothingly.

My mind is racing. How much have I forgotten about my first few months here? What has happened to me? It's a chilling thought. Like waking up after you've been blacked out drunk, not having any clue what happened to you the night before.

"Nothing bad has happened," Nyx says softly when he sees my panic-stricken face.

"How do you know what has happened?" I ask tearfully. "Were you around 24/7? Who knows what has been done to me, how many times I've been fed on. This is terrifying," I cry out.

Alexander comes close to me again, crouching down in front of me. "Baby. You know we run this school," he tells me soothingly. "We would have found out if something had happened. And we've been watching over you for a while, ever since the attacks started. You haven't been alone."

For once I'm grateful for their stalker-like tendencies. I can feel myself relaxing because I can tell they are serious. I haven't been alone.

I feel exhausted. This is so much to take in...so much to think about. Suddenly a thought hits me. I've had sex with two of the vampires. And aren't vampires...

"Are you dead?" I blurt out, shivering at the question since I'm not into the idea of necrophilia in the least bit.

Finn answers this one, shaking his head with a small, amused smile on his far too handsome face. "I think that rumor came from the fact that we don't have souls. So whatever priest was trying to describe us back in the day labeled us as the dead or undead because to them we were veritably dead in the water without a soul. Without a soul there's no path to redemption," he explains. "But to answer your question, we're born just like you. I was a baby...and now I'm grown. We just kind of stop aging after a certain point."

"I saw yearbooks that made it seem like you're quite a bit older than me," I tell him accusingly, wondering if he's lying to me.

The guys exchange looks again. "Don't freak out, okay," says Finn, holding up his hands beseechingly. "We do grow up like you, but like I said...we stop eventually and are kind of frozen like this indefinitely," he explains, gesturing to this god-like body. "We're basically immortal, so schooling and training is kind of an ongoing thing rather than just something you do when you're young. You're not really considered an adult in our society for a few hundred years."

My mouth drops. "How old *are* all of you?" I ask incredulously. "And can you stop doing the side eye thing with each other? It's annoying watching you guys try to talk over my head...wait. Are you telepathic?" I ask, feeling panicked.

Now they all start laughing. "I wish," says Nyx. "I would love to be able to do that."

I breathe a quiet sigh of relief. I really didn't want to think that they'd been able to see all along how infatuated I've been with them since the beginning. That would have been embarrassing.

"To answer your question, Finn and Nyx are the babies of the group, they're both around one hundred," Dante explains. "I'm one hundred and five, and Alexander is a year older. Braxton of course is the oldest at one hundred and ten."

I look at him shocked. It all just keeps getting crazier and crazier. I have a headache building from all the stress and it feels like my brain is going to explode.

"You're basically robbing the cradle then," I finally say with a huff while they all burst out with relieved laughter.

It's so much to take in. I have so many more questions. I open my mouth to ask something else and the room starts to get blurry and spin...and that's about the time I pass out, my poor brain apparently too overwhelmed with everything I have learned to stay awake any longer.

CHAPTER 11

*I*t's hard to concentrate in class, not after the revelation I've just been told. I didn't wake up until right before class, apparently too overwhelmed to join the living for a while after the big reveal. I haven't really talked to the guys about anything as I've had back to back classes. My head still swims with the information overload.

Braxton keeps sending me looks as he can tell that my mind is elsewhere in his class. Aside from finding out that I'm surrounded by vampires who desperately want my soul, there's a twitching sensation that keeps spreading across my shoulder blades and distracting me. I feel a sharp pain often and I wonder if I slept on my back wrong last night. I awkwardly reach behind my back to try to rub the itch, but it doesn't do anything.

Class finally ends, and I stand up from my desk. Clarissa is talking to Braxton, and I can tell that he's anxious to get rid of her and talk to me by the way his eyes keep shifting towards me. After a minute, when there's no way I can cover hanging around without it being awkward, I decide just to leave. I can catch up with Braxton later. Besides, I'm thinking I should lay down based on the fact that my back is starting to hurt worse and worse.

I begin to walk down the hall. But I have to start taking breaks, leaning against the walls until the pain in my back subsides. Something is very wrong. I know that people are looking at me strangely, but I'm feeling too weird to do anything about it. I've just turned down an empty hallway when the twitching intensifies. It feels like my bones are about to break through my skin. The way I'm feeling, there's no way I'm going to make it to my room. I force myself to walk into an empty classroom and find a seat, thinking that I can text one of the guys to help me if it doesn't subside.

Every step to the seat grows harder and harder. I take a step, and then it happens. It feels like my skin is starting to split open across my back. I take a shuddering breath and stop trying to get to the seat. I start to sink to my knees, knowing I can't go any further. Pain slices across my body, so intense that all the air in my lungs rushes out with a great gasp.

A sharp crack coming from my body sounds throughout the room. My knees buckle and I'm forced to the ground, face flush against the stone floor as something shoots out of my back. I hit my head as I fall, and the room spins around me. It takes a moment before I can see well enough to start trying to figure out what just happened. My heart is pounding as panic surges through me. I pull out my phone from the pocket in my skirt and I turn on the camera, switching it to selfie mode so I can see myself better. My face is pale in the camera, beads of sweat are flecked across my forehead. But I can deal with that. It's the silvery white wings extended from behind me that I'm not sure what to do with.

It takes me a while for the image to sink in... like really sink in. Panic is crawling over my flesh.

Wings!

I have freaking wings!

Am I hallucinating?

You have angel blood. Braxton's words roll over my mind.

Fuck!

"Guess this confirms I'm not human," I mutter out loud to myself, even as hysterical laughter starts to swell up in my chest.

Hesitantly, I reach an arm back to touch my new wings, my mind unable to comprehend that they are real. They extend behind me at least three feet, and they're heavy against my back. So heavy that I'm not sure that they have any utility, because I don't see how I could possibly be able to fly with them.

Did I really just think that? Flying?

Maybe I've gone crazy. The school has finally driven me off the deep end. That would explain what I'm seeing. And what I'm feeling. My hand strokes the soft feathers that cover my wings. They're silky and smooth to the touch. They definitely feel real.

Cautiously, like it's an alien I'm touching and not something that's connected to my body, I continue to explore the wings. I shiver at the touch, thinking that it's a ticklish feeling. My heart's beating so fast I'm afraid it's going to burst from my chest. At that thought, my wings give a little flutter behind me.

The move surprises me and I give a little squeak feeling like a fool. I push myself back up, and this time I try to move my wings on purpose. Thinking about moving them doesn't work, so I start trying different things, trying to see if I can elicit any movement. Finally, I concentrate on pushing my energy into where the wings are connected to my body. Blocking everything else out, I put all my focus on that spot. And surprisingly, it works. My wings began to gently move. I'm in awe as I stare at them, which means that I lose focus and they immediately stop moving. Which is probably a good thing, because just then I start to hear voices in the hallway as students start to walk to their classes.

The noises stir me to life, as I remember that I am in a classroom right now. And judging by the lack of dust on the desks, it's one that's used. "Shit, shit, shit," I murmur to myself anxiously as I move my phone from camera mode to the call log. I don't have very many numbers in it, but it feels like it's an important decision who I call to help me right now. My thumb automatically gravitates towards Finn's name. And without another thought I press the call button and wait anxiously as it rings. He doesn't pick up on the first call, and I panic, remembering he's in class at this time.

Just as I'm about to try Alexander's number, my phone buzzes. It's Finn, calling me back. My heart gives a leap as I fumble to accept the call.

Adi?" he asks in a soft concerned voice. "Are you okay?" he whispers. For a second, I'm struck at the fact that he must've left class immediately to call me back. I'm still not used to the way these boys care for me. I've never had anyone care for me like this other than my parents.

"Adi?" he asks again carefully, worry in his tone.

I shake my head, trying to stay focused. I'm not sure why my brain wants to bounce all over the place when I'm in the middle of crisis mode. All right, because I just sprouted wings. Anyone would be a little disoriented after that.

"I need your help," I tell him urgently as I hear more voices coming down the hall. Any minute now someone's going to come in and see me sitting on the floor with giant wings coming out of my back. I'll probably be put into some kind of freakshow exhibit or something. The way the guys have put it, I'm somewhat of a rarity, even in the school filled with vampires. Who knows, maybe whoever found me would just attack me on sight, trying to get a piece of my soul.

"Where are you? I'll come right now," he asks, not grilling me on why I need help, which I'm grateful for.

"The east wing," I tell him. "I'm in the far hallway, in one of the classrooms. I'm not sure which one."

"I'm on my way," he tells me. "Stay on the line."

I hear a whoosh of air, and I know he's using that speed travel thing some of the vampires seem to possess. For once, I'm grateful that he's a vampire with special powers. It would take a human at least twenty minutes to walk over here from where his class is located.

It only takes a few minutes before I hear someone walk in. At first, I'm afraid that it's a student coming into class but the sharp surprising gasp I hear as the person sees my wings sounds more awestruck than surprised. And that's how I know it's Finn.

"Adeline," he whispers, that same worshipful tone in his voice. I haven't looked at him yet, because I'm a little afraid to see his reaction.

I don't think I could stand it if he was looking at me like I was a freak show, even if his voice sounds the opposite of that. More voices in the hallway convince me to look however, as I remember that it's only a matter of time before people walk in.

I regret not looking sooner, because I know the look on his face is one that I'll remember forever. He's looking at me like I'm everything. Like I'm the most precious thing he's ever seen.

My wings start to flutter behind me, like they've seen something that they like. It's weird having something attached to me that's a part of me, but yet separate at the same time.

"Hi," I say lamely, as my cheeks flush under the tender look in his eyes. "I guess you guys were right."

He lets out a chuckle. "I guess so," he says as he begins to approach me in swift strides. He stops short though, and I can tell what he wants based on his hesitation.

"Go ahead and touch them," I say with a laugh.

He throws me a broad grin as he takes the last step towards me and slowly reaches out a hand to stroke one of my wings, moving cautiously like he's approaching a wild animal.

I shiver in delight as he begins to stroke my wings. I almost feel like purring at the sensation. *No wonder dogs like to be petted so much*, I think absentmindedly as I enjoy the light touch of Finn's hands as he worshipfully touches my wings.

Suddenly he freezes, and I can feel the tension building up inside of him. "How will I even begin to get you out of here?" he says frantically. He's to the door in a flash, slamming it shut and pulling a desk in front of it so that no one can come in. He runs his hands through his hair, looking like he's about to throw up.

He pulls out his cell phone, presses the button, the phone to his ear. "You need to get here right now." I can hear someone saying something back to him, but I can't make out who it is. "Far hallway. Third door on the left," he mutters distractedly as he looks at my wings as if they're a problem that needs to be solved, before he drops the phone from his ear.

"What's wrong?" I ask him, the panic I had momentarily quelled at his appearance bursting forth once more.

"We can't let anyone see you like this," he says, beginning to pace.

I didn't want anyone to see me like this, but the way he said it made me think that I would be in actual danger if someone did. Was it that serious?

I begin to ask him, but he holds up his hand to stop me from talking, a very uncharacteristic move as he's always considerate of my feelings.

It only makes me panic more, and my heart is racing now. I awkwardly stand up, the move difficult because of how unbalanced I feel because of my wings.

He stops pacing and stares at me once more, until it seems like he comes to a decision. He's standing in front of me before I can blink my eyes. And then his lips are on me. I'm stiff at first, but I can't help but melt into his embrace as he puts his arms around me, pulling me to him as close as I can get. All thoughts flee from my mind. There's only him. There's only us. I only come back to earth when a sharp knock sounds on the door to the classroom. The sound is jarring in the small room, and with a loud crack my wings burst out, the momentum knocking me into Finn. Somehow while we were kissing my wings had retracted.

"Fuck," Finn groans as he touches our heads together for one more minute before reluctantly pulling away. I realize then that he had kissed me in hopes that I would relax enough for my wings to go back in my body. I move to kiss him again, but he shakes his head, moving towards the door.

"It's Alexander. I better let him in," he says. A second later the desk is moved, and the door is opened and a frantic looking Alexander bursts into the room.

"How long where you going to..." Alexander trails off as he sees me standing there looking like an extra from a Christmas program featuring an angel heralding the second coming.

"I wasn't expecting this," Alexander murmurs in a dazed tone.

"Surprise," I tell him in a falsely positive voice.

It takes him a second, but his eyes sharpen suddenly, the same way that Finn's had when he came to whatever realization he had come to about the presence of my wings. He suddenly slams the door shut behind him, leaning against it, his eyes darting around the room.

"This is bad," he says, flicking his eyes towards Finn who is wearing an anxious expression. "Any ideas of what to do here?" he asks him.

"I found something that worked," Finn answers. "But you kind of scared the wings right out of her again."

"Well, do whatever you did again. We need to get her out of here before someone sees," Alexander barks at him.

Finn just rolls his eyes and pulls me towards him again. And before I can take another breath, he's once again kissing me as if his life depends on it. Or maybe it's my life that is depending on it.

I hear Alexander take a sharp intake of breath at the kiss, but then the whole world fades away again as I soak in the love that is pouring out of Finn. It's so intense and real that it takes my breath away. But all of a sudden, I start to feel lightheaded. It's only after Finn is thrown off of me and I'm caught in Alexander's arms before I fall to the ground, that I realize that Finn had started to feed off me. My wings shoot out once again at the realization. Looks like they don't intend to stay contained any time soon.

I look at where Finn landed. I'm sure surprise, hurt, and horror written across my face. The feeling quickly fades however when I see the pure devastation and agony present on Finn's features. It appears that he hadn't meant to try and feed on me.

"What the fuck, man," Alexander yells at him angrily, forgetting for a minute that we're supposed to be hiding in this room and not attracting any attention.

"Adi, I didn't mean to..." Finn exclaims in a harried voice.

"It's okay," I tell him softly, because I know that Finn hadn't meant to do it. The confusion on his face tells me he has no idea how that just happened.

"It's okay?" Alexander asks incredulously. "Are you crazy? It's the opposite of okay," he continues angrily.

I take a shuddering breath and force myself to stand up. The dizziness is fading, and I feel stronger as each second passes. "Incredible," Alexander murmurs. "You really are something," he says as he watches me.

I quirk an eyebrow. "Is that good?" I ask him.

Alexander just shakes his head and turns his attention back to Finn. "How could you let that happen?" he asks him, fury rolling off of him in waves.

Finn shakes his head, still looking tortured. "I don't know how it happened. I just... I couldn't stop it once it started."

Alexander takes a deep breath. "We'll figure that out later. For now, we've got to get her out of this room," he says as he studies my wings. "I don't think we're going to be able to keep her calm enough to get her to Braxton's room quickly." He thinks for a moment. "Text Nyx," he orders Finn. "Tell him to create a large enough distraction that everyone will be called from their classrooms and into the auditorium immediately."

Finn pulls out his phone again, typing in a few words before setting it down. No one says anything for at least a minute, and I'm about to begin asking questions when all of a sudden, a siren starts ringing in the room. I can hear it out in the hallway as well. It's jarring and out of place in this ancient looking castle. Alexander and Finn look pleased at the sound.

"What's that for?" I ask anxiously as my wings start to move about agitatedly.

Alexander looks distracted, as if he's listening to what's going on out in the hallway. And then I remember that they can hear far better than I can.

"Nyx and Dante got some help from a close friend. They created an illusion that made it seem like the school was being attacked. School protocol mandates that all of the students of the school have to be sheltered in the auditorium until the threat is taken care of by the faculty," Alexander explains. "We should be able to get you through the hallways without issue with all the faculty tied up trying to deal with the illusion."

"Okay. So, we're going out there?" I ask anxiously. Alexander nods, before taking off his blazer and beginning to unbutton the front of his shirt.

"Leave the shirt," Finn snaps. "It's going to attract even more attention if someone sees us in the hallway and you're walking shirtless," he says. Alexander nods and buttons his shirt back up. For some reason I giggle at the thought of what we would look like walking down the hall like that. My wings hidden under the school blazer, sticking up from my back awkwardly. And Alexander walking through the chilly hallways, shirtless. That would be quite the sight.

"Juvenile," Alexander says to me when he hears my laugh, but I can see the smirk he's trying to hide on his face.

Alexander and Finn both situate their blazers on top of my wings. There's no way to make it look at all normal as I don't know how to retract my wings at all beyond getting kissed. So basically, the coats look like they are hanging on an enormous coat rack behind my back.

Alexander looks at the set up dubiously, and then shakes his head. "Hopefully Nyx's plan worked and there's no one in the hallway. There's no way that we can hide this."

"I could always kiss her again," Finn says slyly, taking a step towards me.

"That will only attract more attention if someone appears in the halls and her wings snap out because they startle her."

I roll my eyes, pretending to be annoyed. But I know he's right.

"Let's do this," Finn says after listening at the door for another minute. He moves the desk that had been stacked in front of the door. And I once again note how easy it is for him to do that. Looking back, I realize they weren't that good at keeping their supernatural attributes hidden. They had always been smoother with their movements, faster, stronger, better looking than the average human. It's like my mind had blocked out the possibility that they were more than what they seemed. The joke was on me, because I had also missed the fact that I was more than a human as well.

We slipped into the hallway. Alexander and Finn took turns speeding ahead to check out the hallways we are about to pass through. We are almost to Braxton's room, when an uneasy feeling passes over me. I look over my shoulder and think I see a flash of red disappearing around the corner. A flash of red that looked very similar to Clarissa's hair color.

"I think I just saw something," I whisper to Alexander and Finn urgently.

"Where?" Finn asks.

Before I can say another word, Finn speeds away and around the corner. He's back in no time. "I didn't see anything," Finn reassures me.

I nod, hoping that my eyes were just playing tricks on me. Because why would Clarissa not be in the auditorium with the rest of the students? Would she have noticed that the three of us were missing? Probably. But I can't have that bad of luck, right? And would she have been able to get away that quick?

I send up a prayer that I didn't actually see anything, but the rock residing in my stomach tells me otherwise. At least my wings are still covered by the blazer. If someone did see me, they would just be guessing at what I was hiding on my back. Their first thought wouldn't be that I was an angel.

Right?

I feel like I can finally breathe when we're in the safety of Braxton's room. I pull the blazers off my wings; it's beginning to get uncomfortable with them hanging on them like that. My wings flutter as if they're relieved to have the load off as well. Braxton isn't in the room, I assume that he is with the rest of the staff and students, but I could really use his reassuring presence right now.

Alexander fiddles with his phone as we sit there contemplating the fact that I have wings now. A few minutes pass and I hear the lock on the door being fiddled with. I freeze, and a moment later I see why when Braxton walks through the door. His eyes widen in surprise when he sees me sitting on the edge of his bed, wings still extended behind me. They immediately begin to flutter about, almost flirtatiously. Am I actually pretending that my wings have emotions now? I've officially lost it.

Unlike the others, Braxton doesn't wait for permission. He's next to me in just a few steps, stroking the feathers on my wings in wonder. I once again shiver at the feeling.

"Well, this does complicate things," comments Braxton softly. "But they are a beautiful complication."

I blush as seems to be my constant reaction around Braxton nowadays.

"Do you know what to do about them?" Alexander snaps, a hint of jealousy threaded through his voice. Braxton looks at him amused, like he's watching a little boy have a tantrum. I think he's the only one who can get away with looking at Alexander like that. Not that Braxton really can gloat. He's just as jealous as Alexander most of the time, if not more.

Braxton doesn't answer him, and instead he walks over to his bookshelf and grabs one of the volumes on the third shelf. It's an old book that looks like it's about to fall apart at the seams. He begins to flip through the pages, obviously looking for something. The inscription on the binding is in Latin, so I'm not sure what the title of the book is. He finally stops on the page he wants, tracing the lines with his finger as he reads. He nods his head after finding whatever he was looking for, and snaps the book shut. He then walks over to his liquor cabinet and pulls out a bottle of whiskey.

"Pour me one of those while you're at it," Finn says sarcastically.

Braxton sighs, a sound that conveys the fact that he feels like he's in the presence of idiots. He walks over and hands me the tumbler. "Drink this. It will help you to relax."

I look at the glass dubiously. But I guess kissing kind of worked, and that helped me to relax. Maybe this will work even better.

I throw back the drink, the liquid setting my throat on fire. I cough as it burns my throat, but I can already feel myself relaxing as a fuzzy warmth spreads through my limbs.

Braxton takes the glass once again and I look at him in alarm. "Is the goal for me to get so drunk that I pass out?" I ask as he pours another sizable amount.

"I've been doing research since I found out what you were," he explains. "Until you learn how to retract your wings, the only way for us to help you keep them out of sight is to keep you relaxed."

"You know, it's kind of ironic that I'm supposedly an angel and the way for me to hide my wings is to get drunk," I respond wryly. "But I guess kissing didn't work very well, so we'll see if this does any better," I say while taking the glass. Braxton's eyes flash dangerously. "Kissing?"

I snort at his response and toss the drink back. Sure enough, I soon become aware that the weight on my back is easing, and the wings have slipped out of sight. I'm still somehow aware of their presence right under my skin, ready to come out at any moment.

Braxton looks satisfied that it had worked. He's about to say something else when we hear a buzzing noise signaling that his phone is going off. I feel a flicker of unease as Alexander realizes that his phone is also buzzing. Braxton and Alexander look at each other.

"The Council wants to see us," Braxton says in an alarmed tone.

"Clarissa," I whisper to myself, but of course the guys all hear me with their supersonic hearing.

The guys look at me questioningly.

"That's who was in the hallway. That's what I saw. Her hair. She must've gone straight to the Council after she saw us." I feel the panic trying to undo the calmness I have been feeling from the whiskey.

I feel my shoulder blades begin to tingle as my wings threaten to make a reappearance. I take deep breaths trying to calm myself down. Braxton sees how worried I am, and he too takes a deep breath. "It will be okay. They're not going to believe Clarissa over Alexander and me. I've got fifty years of loyal Council service. And Alexander's been including Clarissa's jealous behavior towards you in his reports. Everything's going to be fine."

He's trying to sound reassuring, but his voice sounds frightened. I've seen firsthand just how persuasive Clarissa can be. The guys haven't told me just what being an angel means as far as the vampire council goes. But by the way they're acting, I'm quite sure that I don't want to find out.

"They're asking for our presence right now," says Alexander, putting his blazer back on that we had used to help cover my wings. "Finn, stay here with Adeline. Be ready to get her out of here if things take a turn," he tells him seriously.

Finn stands up straighter, and nods, an intense gleam in his eyes that tells me that he'll get me out of here whether I want to leave or not.

"You don't think you'll be in danger, right?" I ask worriedly, thinking about the Council's reaction if they find out that Alexander and Braxton are hiding something from them.

Braxton flashes me a fake smile. "Of course not. We're more than capable of looking out for ourselves," he tells me reassuringly.

My wings fly out again at his statement, and the timing of it makes everyone in the room chuckle, momentarily alleviating the stifling tension that surrounds us. Alexander and Braxton both give me succinct kisses before leaving the room. I send up another prayer, hoping that the fact that I am an angel meant that whoever is up there would maybe listen and keep them safe.

Finn walks over and grabs the bottle that Braxton had been using before.

"Let's try this again," he says as he pours me another glass.

It's going to be a long wait.

CHAPTER 12

(BRAXTON)

*T*here's excitement in the air when we walk into the cavernous Council room. I know immediately that Adeline was right, someone had seen her walk to my room. The excitement stems from the fact that the vampires are looking forward to having another feeding source. It sickens me to think that a few months ago I might have been feeling the same way.

I look around the room and note that the only beings present are the Council, Alexander and myself, and Clarissa. She's looking at us with pride gleaming in her eyes. She thinks she has us.

I just hope we can actually pull this off. I wouldn't think that members of the Council would go there, but there's always the chance that Clarissa has her fangs stuck into at least a few of the members.

"I assume that you know why you've been sent for?" Elliott Culpepper asks.

Dante walks in just then, my heart starts to beat faster. I can only hope that his allegiance to Adeline means more to him then getting approval from his father. His presence also means that the Council has been watching us closer than we thought. I'm just hoping that they haven't called Finn and Nyx to make an appearance. I don't want to leave Adeline alone.

I school my face and concentrate on getting my heartbeat down to its normal rhythm. The Council will be looking for signs of anything out of the ordinary.

"Is this about the fake attack earlier?" I ask, working on keeping my voice steady. Elliot gives me a searching glance. He thinks that I'm hiding something, and it's only my reputation and years of service that's keeping me safe right now.

"Clarissa has come to us with some interesting news about Miss Jones," Elliott says, pausing once again to try and read my reaction.

"And what would that be?" Alexander asks in a bored voice. "I haven't quite figured out Clarissa's obsession with the girl."

Elliott turns his focus to Alexander for a moment, searching his features to see if there's anything out of the ordinary. But Alexander's mastered the poker face, just the same as me. Even Dante's doing a great job of looking bored as he lounges against the cavern wall.

Elliott is beginning to look a bit flustered. I guess he was assuming this was going to go a different way. I can see out of the corner of my eye that Clarissa's face is starting to get red.

Principal Asher interjects. "Clarissa is telling us that we have an angel on our hands," he says, his eyes gleaming greedily.

"An angel?" Alexander says dramatically, like this is the most surprising news that he's ever gotten. He starts to laugh uproariously. A clever move, since none of the men in this room like to be laughed at. Principal Asher looks flustered.

"Adeline Jones is the farthest thing from an angel that I've ever seen. The Council needs to get better sources if they're going to waste my time with things like this," I tell them in a bored tone as Alexander continues to laugh.

"What the hell are you laughing at?" shrieks Clarissa.

"Just the fact that anyone would listen to you," Alexander says venomously. "Everyone knows that you're obsessed with her. You couldn't come up with a better story than this? You might as well pretend that you're pregnant and it's mine," Alexander says snarkily.

Elliott straightens himself up, trying to get in control of the situation. "Alexander, we've had you watching her. You really haven't seen anything out of the ordinary?" he presses.

Alexander pretends to think. "If by out of the ordinary you mean exceptionally self-righteous? Then Miss Jones is your girl," he says with a mean-spirited laugh.

The Council members are beginning to look a little bit embarrassed about their accusations in the face of our sarcasm.

"They're lying," Clarissa says desperately, her eyes darting frantically around the room, trying to see if anyone believes her. "They're all obsessed with her. Braxton's fucking her. Hell, they all probably are."

There's an intake of breath at her accusation and I know I'm treading on dangerous ground now. Surprisingly it's Alexander's mother that pipes up before I can say a word. "Are you accusing my son of having relations with a human?" she asks Clarissa menacingly.

Clarissa takes an audible gulp at the threat in the council woman's voice. "I..." She takes a deep breath, steeling herself and bracing her shoulders. "Yes, I am as a matter of fact."

The room erupts, everyone talking over themselves as they discuss this new development. Alexander and I sneak looks at each other.

"It's funny you should say that, Clarissa," Dante says suddenly. "For someone that's fucking a professor yourself, you would think you would know to have proof when leveling accusations like that. You do know that something like that would violate about a million different Raven Academy rules," he says with a smirk.

"I don't know what you're talking about," Clarissa throws back, even as the room starts to get loud again in the face of yet another accusation.

I'm holding my breath that Dante has something concrete to get us out of this mess. I watch as he pulls out his phone and walks towards his stepmother, holding it out for her to take. She sends him a questioning glance before taking the phone and pressing something on it. Suddenly the sound of Clarissa and Dusk groaning and moaning fills the cavern. Alexander's mother looks horrified at what she's seeing, and she quickly presses something to make the recording stop playing.

She tosses Dante his phone and stands up so fast that her chair topples to the ground behind her.

"I believe we're done here. Make sure Dusk is out of the school within the hour," she orders as she begins to walk away, trying to hold her head high even in her obvious embarrassment that the Council even called this meeting to begin with based on Clarissa's accusations. She stops, as if she's just remembered something. "Clarissa, make sure your bags are packed as well," she says stiffly before storming off.

Clarissa looks pale, but it's not from worry or embarrassment about what has just happened, it's from rage.

She turns to look at us as the rest of the Council begin to file out of the room. She doesn't stop staring at us even when they've all left. There's determination in her gaze and tendrils of unease spread all over my skin. She has some kind of plan. And it's not going to be good for us.

We may have won this battle, but it's obvious that Clarissa is determined to win the war.

* * *

(Adeline)

I'm walking down the hall with Nyx and Finn, a bit unsteadily, when Clarissa suddenly storms to a stop in front of me. For some reason, I had thought that it was a good idea to try and go to class drunk with the danger of my wings popping out at any moment. Nyx and Finn hadn't been that far off from my intoxication level so it had been an easy sell that I couldn't afford to put my academic future in jeopardy over something as simple as a pair of angel wings.

We obviously weren't thinking straight.

Clarissa gets so close to me that her nose is only inches away from my forehead. "Listen you little bitch, it's only a matter of time until everyone knows your secret. I'll make sure of that," she hisses.

I wobble in front of her, almost falling into her. "What are you talking about and why are there two of you," I giggle, vaguely aware that she's threatening me about something important, but too drunk to care. Maybe giving me enough alcohol to lay down an elephant in order to get my wings to relax wasn't the best idea.

Clarissa sniffs me and looks at me incredulously. "Are you drunk right now?" she asks in shock.

Nyx and Finn just laugh in response. "Are you all drunk?" she asks wide-eyed.

She begins to laugh. The sound is distorted in my hazy mind, sounding more like a cartoon villain's laugh then a real person's... "This is too good. The entire supernatural world is plotting what to do with you and you're getting drunk with two of your harem. You're making it too easy, Adeline. Why don't you give me a little challenge?"

Her words are beginning to sober me up. I have no idea what she's threatening to do, but it's obvious she knows more about me than she should.

* * *

(Clarissa)

"Fuck off, Clarissa," Nyx growls, pulling Adeline tight under his arm like she's a fragile ornament. "I'm so sick of your jealousy," he barks.

Finn is on her other side, both watching over her.

That whining little cow stares at me with drunken glazed eyes, half giggling, half rubbing herself up against Finn. I want to smash my fist into that perfect little nose, to remind her that her place at this Academy is beneath our shoes. We rule this place, not humans or anyone else.

"Whoaaa. I know you have fantasies but keep them to yourself," I snap at Nyx, lifting my chin in his direction.

But he's already turning away, taking Adeline and Finn with him, and I can't keep looking at them without wanting to gag.

I storm off in the opposite direction, clenching my fists, my tongue slipping over my extending fangs, the tips pointy and sharp. On her first day Adeline walked in on me and my sexy Dusk, I should have torn her throat out then been done with her. *Stupid, stupid, stupid.* Won't make that mistake again.

I now know her secret, and I'm doing what I should have done before.

Something that will not only eliminate her but also serve as payback for those arrogant assholes who think they're too good for me. Traitors who put a damn angel before their own kind.

Recently, I heard the nurses talking about a command to take Adeline's blood for Council testing, which was bewildering enough. I kept wondering what they'd want with a human's blood, but now it all makes sense.

Seeing her trying to conceal her wings in the hallway.

And those four grovelers and Braxton chasing after her 24/7.

She's a damn angel. Can't believe I didn't see this earlier based on her freakish show of strength that day in the hallway and the crazy way that the other vampires in the school acted towards her. Her kind are almost extinct on Earth because down here, they are weak and at our mercy.

Vampires rule this world.

My grandparents kept an angel as a slave to clean the house and to be fed upon. They managed that by clipping her wings, literally chopping them right off her. This was many years ago, and the snippets I remember were of the young woman in her twenties pleading for her life every day. But grandma told me something very important.

Angels affect everyone around them, influence their emotions with a strange pheromone-type energy. *It brings out the truth in someone's heart,* Grandma used to say. *Sweeps into unsuspecting hearts like a siren. Elicits such powerful emotions in everyone they encounter. So care must be taken.*

Never let angels get too close to you.

They will change you, deceive you.

Angels are good for one thing--food.

Then Grandma fed on the angel, drinking in her soul until the angel passed out, like she did most days. The thing was, if Vampires fed on humans too long, the humans' souls can rapture and break since humans already have cracks in their soul from the fall of Adam. But angels on the other hand can be fed on without destroying their soul as they have the purest, most whole souls of any beings on Earth. It makes them the ultimate food source.

Except, there's a double-edged sword with angels and it comes with a downside my grandma didn't see before it was too late. She fed on the girl so frequently, the angel finally died. Soon after, my grandma died also. Her addiction for angel blood had driven her insane to the point where she finally took her own life to stop the excruciating hunger.

So, if those idiots are feeding on Adeline, they've just screwed themselves royally. But I can live with that.

Fuck them!

I push myself into a run down the hall for one reason. The nurse confided in a friend that Adeline's blood samples had been swapped with human blood since she smelled the difference and was too scared to tell the Council. And I bet my life I know exactly who took it and where it is now.

Her lover boy...the only one who'd have easy access to the nurse's room after hours.

As I reach Braxton's door, I pause and listen for any sounds coming from inside.

Silence.

He's a fool to not have more locks on his room to prevent people from entering easily, but yay for me. I rush inside and do a quick scan to confirm that I'm alone in the bedroom, then I jump toward his study desk and shuffle through the papers on the desk. I rip open the drawers, one after another and come up short. No blood sample.

Hell. I whip around and sprint across the room, hopping up and over his bed to the wardrobe and yank open the door.

Pants and shirts perfectly pressed hang in perfect order by colors from blacks to grays, whites, blues, and greens.

I snort a laugh at how anal he is and shove aside the clothes, searching for anything toward the back of the wardrobe. Nothing, and there are only shoes at the base. Useless.

Where would he hide the blood sample. I eye the bedside table and search the drawer finding only books and a reading light, along with a box of condoms.

"Too bad he wastes those on Adeline." I shove the drawer shut with my hip and lift the edge of the mattress, finding nothing.

Am I wrong to think he'd hide it instead of destroying the evidence immediately?

I search every corner of the room until I look behind the small two-seater eating table and discover a small bar fridge.

Mr. Dusk has his filled with all kinds of blood types for when I spend nights with him so we can gorge, and I assumed it was only him who had such a luxury in his room.

I lunge forward and wrench open the door, my gaze shooting to one blood sample in a test tube inside a plastic bag. My fading hopes jack up inside me, and I'm smiling.

"Fuck yeah, bitch. You're done."

I hear voices outside the room; Finn and Nyx. Concentrating, my ears perk as I focus and note they're farther down the hall, the footsteps of three people coming closer. Bet that bitch is still with them.

Snatching the blood sample, I stuff it into the pocket of my school skirt and kick the fridge door shut. I dart outside with the speed that makes us a superior race. A quick glance over my shoulder, I catch the guys' shadows rounding the corner of the corridor, and I run out of there, beaming with satisfaction.

I can't wait to see how Alexander and the others are going to try protecting Adeline now.

The always perfect Alexander, with his powerful family... he's about to see his life come crumbling down around him and I can't wait for the showdown.

And once I've dealt with Adeline, I'll enjoy having power restored in the Academy.

Vampires feeding on the fresh new recruits coming into our school as a smorgasbord, none of them special.

Finally, Alexander will see me as the only one for him as it should have been all along.

I move with speed towards the Council's room and burst inside without knocking.

A startled Elliot turns in my direction, his mouth twisted, eyes furious. "Have you completely forgotten your place? Aren't you supposed to be packing?"

"I apologize for the intrusion, but this can't wait. You'll want to see what I have for you," I respond smugly. With my hand in my pocket, fingers curling around the blood sample, I march toward the Councilman feeling like right now, I can take on the world.

Yep, things are going to get very interesting now.

* * *

(Nyx)

I take quick steps out of Braxton's room and head towards the vending machines. After all that alcohol, Adeline's feeling queasy, and eating something will help her.

Students are roaming the hallways, blissfully going about their business, many totally unaware of all that goes on in this school. My lips quirk just thinking about the fact that there's been an angel walking these halls without anyone knowing. A being that the vampire students would do anything to claim as their own if they knew.

Adeline is unbelievably special, and it surprises me she's gone undetected for this long. I'm just glad that we all came to our senses in time to be able to work together to keep her safe.

Fuck everything else. All that matters now is Adeline, and that's all I concern myself with.

Further down the hall, there's movement that catches my eyes. I glance down the long corridor and spot Clarissa shutting the door that leads to the Council's den. She's practically skipping, wearing a huge grin, and my gut clenches. The only time she smiles that way is when she's done something awful.

I slide into an empty classroom and peer out the door, waiting for her to pass, not wanting her to know I saw where she came from. She's licking her lips as she strolls past, and I'm itching to deliver violence her way, to make her talk. But she won't tell me anything. The bitch will probably get turned on by my attempts. I want to gag.

The moment she's out of sight, I dart out and reach the Council's door in two seconds.

Curiosity is a bastard, so I'm leaning closer, pressing my ear to the door like a damn spy. Focusing, I listen to the voice coming faintly from inside.

"Yes, you heard right," Elliot quips, and when I don't hear a response, I'm guessing he's on the phone. "I have actual proof."

Proof of what? My gut is tightening with each passing second, each agreeing sound he makes. I don't want to think they are talking about Adeline. Braxton, Dante, and Alexander said we had time, that they had thrown the Council off the scent of Adeline.

I'm still picturing Clarissa's maniacal grin after leaving Elliot's office.

"Yes, that's what I'm saying, you need to get here fast. I just tested the blood myself. She has the ey' compound. She's what we've been looking for!"

At his words, I die on the inside, and I can't move at first as the realization of what I've just heard sinks in.

Clarissa somehow found the blood sample that Braxton had swiped from the nurse's office and ran with it to Elliot.

Now that bastard has called the Council back to take Adeline...my angel.

Tiny hairs on the back of my neck rise, and the terror is tangible in the air around me, so heavy I can taste it in the wake of this horrendous news.

I'm grinding my teeth, and everything falls silent around me as fear of what I'm about to lose sinks through me.

We're supposed to protect Adeline, but this...That fucking bitch, Clarissa. I'm going to murder her.

First things first though, I move with purpose, racing with incredible speed, not caring who sees me as I head back for Adeline.

We need to get her out of the school now!

CHAPTER 13

(ALEXANDER)

"*I*f they find out, Adi's as good as dead," Dante murmurs at my back in the school hallway.

I turn, my jaw clenches. There's always been something about Dante that just rubs me the wrong way. He might be my step-brother, but who says family has to get along? Except he basically saved us in that meeting, and he has a point I agree with for a change. In truth, it isn't Dante I'm furious with, but Clarissa. I want to rip her damn head off.

"You think I don't know that?" I growl in response. "We need a plan to deal with the Council permanently and keep Adi safe, at any cost. You know what they'll do to her if they take her?"

His lips pinch tight and he nods, the corded muscles in his neck tensing. "What's the plan then? We take her away from here? They know who her family is though, and we can't hide her forever."

Fury floods my system, mixed with a desperate urgency. Time is ticking. The Council has a whiff of an angel at the school, and they'll be relentless in uncovering the truth. What just happened back there is just a temporary fix. There's a reason most of the angels assigned to live on Earth have perished, why so few have taken their places.

But Adi...my chest squeezes...I'll defy my own kind to protect her. I'll do whatever it takes.

"I'll think of something," I answer.

"We need to tackle Clarissa before the news spreads beyond the Council." Dante's seething, his face burning up with anger, and he isn't controlling it well.

"Blow off some steam, and we'll talk later when I get everyone together."

Dante makes a growling sound under his breath and suddenly takes a sharp left and marches away, his shoulders curled forward. I feel that same fear sitting heavily on me too...fear for Adi and losing her.

I push back the rage threatening to swallow me and stride down the hallway to the cafeteria, hoping to find Clarissa. Payback is going to be a bitch for her. Her life will be a living hell for crossing me.

I make my way into the half empty food hall and before I take two steps inside, laughter fills the room.

Adi swings to my thoughts, but she's not here, the source is a brunette with her friends talking over their meals. Behind her I spot Connor strolling my way, all smug, and my teeth grind together.

"Have you seen, Adi?" he asks upon approach like we're suddenly friends.

"She isn't your concern," I snarl, scanning the room to find no sign of Clarissa.

"Her and I have a past, so she'll always be my concern."

My stomach tightens as his words linger on my mind. I stare at the empty tables near the corner where Adi used to sit when she first started Raven Academy. But the more I replay Connor's words in my mind, the more anger surges through me. He single handedly took down Dixon and I saw him fight that fuckhead... I take a sniff of the air around me, of him and he carries no scent, concealing everything. But I sense a power in the air, rippling over my skin.

I swing my attention to Connor. "What exactly are you?" I hiss the words through clenched teeth.

"Still trying to work it out?" he snorts a laugh.

But I don't miss the sharpening of his gaze, how he deftly scans the room with a sweep of its entirety in a split second. He isn't just something I don't understand, but a warrior, a fighter, an enemy who's entered the wolf den in sheep's clothing.

"Good luck with that," he continues as he steps away.

A blazing fury is roaring through me, and any control I held onto is now slipping.

I reach for the back of his head and snatch the nape of his neck with force, but he pivots on a heel as if expecting my reaction, rips from my grip and crouches low before swinging a leg that slams into the side of my knees. I stumble, feet slipping backward as I'm caught off guard, which isn't like me.

I release a savage growl.

His face is perfectly in control, all except for the fine lines bracketing the corners of his mouth, deepening with his agitation. He shoves me backward, and he's on me in seconds, faster than any mere human should move, his fist flying for my face. The surprise of his speed has me reacting slower than I should, and his punch connects with the side of my face, sending a shudder through my skull.

The room around us explodes with cheers from the crowd closing in around us, but I don't give a fuck.

"I'm giving you one chance to leave Adi alone," Connor warns me.

I break out laughing at the insolence of this... whatever the fuck he is.

I'll tear him apart.

My eyes settle on him, feet from me, still as silence, practiced in the hunt.

His eyes darken. "You think I don't know what you are. I'm not scared, I'm excited to show you what I can do."

I shoot forward, sick of hearing his mumbling threats when he has no idea who I am.

His eyes widen for a sliver of a heartbeat before we clash, delivering blow after blow. I'll show him why I'm feared, why *he'll* fear me.

We're rolling on the floor and crash into a table. He shoves me off him, before kicking me in the gut, inches above my groin.

He scrambles to his feet, smirking and knowing too well he'd meant to hit me a bit lower. Bastard plays dirty.

Swiping his mouth, blood streaks his cheek and hand, and I inhale the scent... human. Not possible, not with his strength and speed.

Students are roaring around us when Connor comes at me, his shoulder slamming into my gut with the force of a mountain. My feet slip backward, and I grab the table near me, lifting it over my head and hurl it at him.

He's a rat, moving so damn fast, diving into a roll, the table missing him by a fraction of an inch. But I rush after him, and we stumble, exchanging punches, and nothing will stop us.

Rage rumbles deep in my chest, noticing the oohs around us have died as everyone stares at me. Students who don't know what I am or my strength, and fuck this isn't the place to kick Connor's ass.

I snatch him by his shirt and hurl him toward the doorway of the cafeteria and out into the hall.

He skids across the ground on his ass until he slams into the lockers. I sprint to him and snatch him by an arm, tossing him farther down the hall like a rag doll, and I dart after him before the students from the cafeteria even emerge to follow us.

He's grumbling, but the dick is already on his feet, raising his fists, hair and school uniform ruffled.

Who the fuck is this guy?

He throws a punch, but I duck my head and swing around behind him and shove my fists into his back, driving him down another corridor and out of sight of the curious busybodies pouring out of the food hall.

"Is that the only way you know how to fight?" he snarls, while the grin pulling at his lips can only be described as feral.

But at least we are out of view from everyone else. So I attack. We come together in an explosion of fists and growls and fury. I need Connor out of my path and Adi's life for good.

He battles sly, dodging my blows, swinging low and darting around me.

I charge and snatch him around the neck with my arm, his head tucked against my side, and I squeeze. "I can snap your neck in two seco--"

I holler as the bastard bites down on my side, tearing flesh through my shirt, wriggling free, and I lunge after him, boiling with anger when a shadow rushes into the corridor with us. It takes me a couple of quick moments to clear my head and focus when Connor drives a fist to the side of my head, sending me reeling into a wall.

"You fucking little shit." I swing around as Finn steps into my line of sight.

"Get out of my way," I roar.

"It's Adi," he says, his voice firm and fearful. I see the fright in his eyes, in the way he's fidgeting with his hair.

My throat goes dry.

"What's wrong with Adi?" Connor asks, stealing the exact words I'm about to voice.

"Stay out of it," I warn, then turn to Finn. "Take me to her."

We're running down the hall, Connor's faint steps close behind, but I don't have time for him, not if something happened to Adi.

"The Council has just arrived back at the Academy." Finn's words fall to a whisper, and I hear the trepidation in his voice.

I clench my fists, fuming that Elliot called them to gather again. Furious that I didn't see this coming so fast. They aren't taking any chances if an angel is in question, and I'm running faster, my feet pounding the solid floor, darting around staring students who are like fucking deer in headlights. No wonder humans are so damn easy to kill. Except the pest on my heels it seems.

"This way," Finn says, and careens left, and I follow him directly to Braxton's room where we left her.

I burst into the room.

Adeline flinches on my arrival, her tucked wings snapping out, knocking Nyx in the head. Her face blanches as she looks at us pushing into the room while Finn shuts us in.

Connor is by my side, his eyes stretched into discs at seeing Adi's wings. "You look...you look stunning. Wow, Adi."

"Stop drooling," I mumble. "Why did you let him in here?" I growl at Finn, who simply shrugs like he can't be bothered to fight the matter, but instead approaches Adeline and reaches out to cup her face. He adores her as much as the rest of us do.

"What's going on?" she asks, glancing from each of us lingering in Braxton's room, staring at her... "And what in the world happened to you two?"

Only then do I pay attention to Connor's busted lip, the bruise forming under his eye, his top missing half the buttons. I grin, liking my handy work. He glances over at me with a death glare.

"That's not important," I say. "We need to get you to safety. The Council has arrived to take you. Evidently they changed their mind about not believing Clarissa."

"The Council's coming to get me? To take me where?"

"Away, baby," Finn coos. "Away from us, from your parents, from everyone."

"No," her voice trembles. She curls in on herself, her wings pulling in tight, surrounding her and Finn in their own little cocoon.

"Where are we going to take her?" Nyx asks.

"Somewhere no one will find her," I say. "Nyx, grab the blankets to conceal her wings. Connor, you might as well make yourself useful and go track down Braxton and Dante. Bring them here right away."

To my surprise, he follows my order and heads out quickly.

I approach my angel and run gentle fingers over her white wings. They are so beautiful, whiter than the purest snow, glinting like luminous diamonds. They are made of long silk-like feathers, and I trace one, feeling it tremble under my touch.

"Adi, we need to leave. It's the only way I can keep you safe."

Her wings shiver and they slowly part away from around her, revealing her cradled in Finn's arms, tears falling down her cheeks. Finn looks at me with dread, with worry for her, and I'm breaking on the inside. It tortures me to even think the Council will get their hands on her, feed on her, and eventually kill her. I shake with fury how my mind drowns with those images. But I can't say those words to Adeline, I can't terrify her more than she already is.

"I know you're scared," I say and gently take her hand until she pulls her head from Finn's chest and looks up at me. "We're all scared," I say. "But you've got all of us fighting for you. We'll fight to the end to protect you. I give you my word. I swear it on my life, on all of our lives."

Tears rivet down her face, and my heart is shattering right now to see the agony and fear in her eyes. My nerves are in hyperdrive at the dread pounding into me. But I hold it together for my angel.

I pull her against me, wrap my arms around her, and hold her. Let her know that no matter what, she isn't alone. That for her, we're ready to go to war.

CHAPTER 14

(ADELINE)

Connor is back with Braxton and Dante in just a few minutes. Braxton doesn't say anything to us, he heads straight towards his fridge. I'm thinking it's an odd time to get a drink, but then I see the panic on his face when he opens the door to the fridge and sees its contents.

"Fuck," he roars, picking up the fridge and throwing it against the wall.

I jump at his anger. I've never seen him like this.

"What happened?" snaps Alexander.

"Either Clarissa or someone from the Council has been in here. Adeline's blood is gone."

"You didn't destroy it?" growls Connor. Braxton shoots him a hate-filled look. "Not that it's any of your business, but I thought we could study it more to understand her genetic makeup better."

"You're an idiot," hisses Connor and Alexander actually looks like he agrees.

"Can you all stop! The blood's gone. End of story. What do we do next?" I ask sternly, sick of the constant fighting.

"We've got to get you out of here. It won't take long for the Council to test your blood and find the ey' compound. They'll be scouring the place for you any minute now," says Braxton in a some-what panicked voice.

"I know how we can get her out," Connor pipes up, and I look at him hopefully.

"He does know the castle even better than I do," admits Alexander begrudgingly.

"Let's go. We'll go out through the tunnels. It's not far from a car I have hidden," says Connor

"They'll be blocking the parking lot," states Nyx.

"I hid my car somewhere else," says Connor in a "how stupid do you think I am" kind of tone. I can almost sense the respect building in the room towards Connor right now. He has a lot of explaining to do, but it looks like he's going to be our savior for the time being.

Nyx opens the door to the hallway, looking both ways before step-ping out. Connor starts to lead us down the hall and around the corner, the guys zipping ahead to scope out who's in the hallway.

"Clarissa's coming," says Alexander suddenly, sniffing the air urgently. Apparently, she has a specific smell.

Dante picks me up and throws me over his shoulder. The walls start to zoom past us as they use their special speed. I'm really hoping that angels have something like that and that it kicks in soon.

Connor stops us at an empty wall down in the wing where Mercy and I had once spied on the "non-scholarship kids" fighting. It seems like a lifetime ago. He presses a stone down near his left knee and a passageway appears. I shiver as I see how dark it is inside. I swallow my fear though; I know these men will do anything they can to keep me safe.

We walk in the tunnel that lies beyond the wall. We're only a few steps in, and Connor has just closed the wall opening when the guys freeze. "They're down here. They must be tracking us. We're fucked if they know about this tunnel," Dante hisses.

"Shhh," Braxton orders and we all fall silent as we listen. Or they listen...I can't hear anything through the thick stone wall.

After a few minutes, they must think that whoever it was has kept going because we start jogging down the tunnel. I start to shiver, a mixture of panic and cold hitting me. My wings suddenly start to flap around. "Ouch," Alexander hisses as they sock him in the face.

"Sorry," I whisper as the others snort. At least we can still find some humor in the situation we've found ourselves in.

It seems to take forever, but finally we get to another wall. Connor hits something on the wall and an opening appears, right in the middle of the forest. Night has fallen and I almost wish we could stay in the tunnel with how eerie the woods are tonight.

"It's around here somewhere," Connor says walking forward. After five minutes of walking, I'm convinced we're lost.

Suddenly Connor stops and points. "It's behind that cluster of trees," he calls out quietly, pointing ahead to what looks like some kind of boulder. The boulder ends up being his car that's been covered with a camo colored cover to help keep it hidden. Not that he was particularly worried about it being discovered. We're in a part of the woods that I bet almost no one has been to.

The rest of the guys help him uncover the car. Connor shines his light just beyond the car, showing a grown over path that looks like it used to be some kind of rudimentary road.

"This used to be where they would smuggle in alcohol during Prohibition. Apparently one of the human students back then helped hide whiskey to make money," Connor explains. "You vamps never paid him any attention," he continues with a wide smile.

However, the road came to be, it's been long forgotten. Looking at Connor's car, it's only a small sedan. My wings are never going to fit in it.

Braxton must see the worry on my face because he laughs and hands me a flask that he pulls from his pocket. "Drink this. Hopefully we can get your wings to retract. They'll never fit in the car."

I nod and guzzle down the whiskey. I cough once again as it burns. I'm never going to get used to the taste. Maybe we should invest in some fruit flavored alcohol.

It takes a minute, but my wings finally retract and we all pile into the car. I'm sitting in Braxton's lap in the front seat as there's not enough seats for everyone. "Breathe," he whispers in my ear. I let out a shaky exhale, nervous that someone is going to stop us at any moment.

We're all silent as Connor drives us down the road, the car rattling as it goes over branches and rocks. I'm expecting a tire to blow out anytime from how rough the road is.

There's a palpable sigh of relief when we finally get to the main road twenty minutes later. "This is ten miles from the entrance of that parking lot you all use. They'll probably have scouts everywhere, but at least they won't be expecting this car or for us to come out this way," Connor says.

I nod gratefully, too exhausted to say anything at the moment. I reach over and squeeze his hand though, and he shoots me a look loaded with what almost looks like love. I quickly retract my hand, not knowing how to respond. To terrified right now to feel anything but my pounding heart.

We drive for hours and hours, only stopping for gas which we pay for with cash. The guys take turns driving and sleeping so we can keep going. I switch who I'm sitting on so it's not too uncomfortable for the guys.

We don't stop until we get to Florida. We don't have a plan at the moment, and the guys haven't really talked despite the long hours we've spent together on the road. Each of them has lost their entire lives and futures in a matter of a day. It's hard for me to swallow down the guilt I'm feeling about everything they have given up for me.

We somehow end up on the beach, right as the sun is rising, and it feels like a new beginning. I stand in the sand, wrapped in Finn's arms with the others around me.

I'm not sure who I am or why my life journey brought me to these men. But I somehow know that we're meant to love each other, to provide solace and an ease to our troubled hearts.

I look up at the same time as Finn tips his head down to capture my mouth with his. He tries for soft, but we're too hungry for slow. We bite away at the horror of the last few days and in the depth of this kiss is our pledge. Our flawed fairytale is full of happy and sad, good and bad, and through it all I have to believe we'll all stay together from here on out.

There can be no other end for us.

TO BE CONTINUED IN SCHOOL OF BROKEN WINGS.
GET YOUR COPY HERE: books2read.com/schoolofbrokenwings

SNEAK PEEK

Keep reading for a sneak peek at The Naughty List, a fun and sexy contemporary standalone.

THE NAUGHTY LIST

C. R. Jane & Mila Young

COPYRIGHT

THE NAUGHTY LIST

We're going to spend the holidays getting me on Santa's Naughty List!

I've always been on the 'Nice' list. Never been one to stray too far from the beaten path, and managed to make it to senior year without doing well... much of anything. Until I ended up stranded in Chicago during the worst snowstorm of the century, away from my family, and days before Christmas.

And then I meet them.

Two of the most insanely gorgeous guys I'd ever laid eyes on.

Charismatic. Sexy. Daring.

I've wanted to escape my life for Christmas for so long...and they offer me a chance I just can't pass up.

What else is a girl going to do while stranded in a strange city on her own?

They insist that they can get me into Santa's Naughty list in less than three days.

So I accept the challenge.

But that's if I can keep my heart... I mean head, in the game.

Because losing my heart was never part of the rules...

NAUGHTY LIST #1: GET DRUNK IN THE MIDDLE OF THE DAY

"Flight 793 to Chicago, will be boarding soon. Please make sure that you have all of your belongings with you," a robotic airline employee's voice said over the intercom.

It was Christmas break, something I'd been dreading the whole semester since it meant that I'd be returning home. A home that was the epitome of hell ever since my father had decided to remarry a woman who I was pretty sure doubled as Maleficent in her spare time. Add in her psychotic son and we were set to have a holly, jolly Christmas.

I picked up my shoulder bag and made sure that my carry-on was still in one piece. I had the luggage forever, and one of the zippers was broken. I was forever worried that all of my underwear was going to spill out in the middle of the airport one day...yet I never bothered to get a new one from a lack of funds.

I began to walk over to the gate entrance. I was one of those people that even though my zone would be one of the last called, I had to be ready. Flight anxiety I guess.

As I weaved through the rows of chairs, I couldn't help but notice some eye-candy sitting over by the windows.

Eye-candy didn't really do them justice though. I was reasonably sure they were the most attractive guys I had ever seen. They were about as far apart in looks as possible. One was a blonde Adonis while the other one looked like a fallen angel with hair so dark that it almost looked blue under the airport's bad lighting.

They looked like they had been carved from marble with their bodies that were so good even under their clothes that I wasn't sure if they were real...I was drooling. I hadn't thought it was possible to actually see a six-pack through clothes, but the proof was right in front of me.

The dark-haired dreamboat caught me staring just then and shot me a wink with piercing blue eyes that threatened to do me in. I quickly averted my eyes and walked faster to where people were starting to gather to get in line. I could feel a hot blush creeping up my neck at the fact that he had seen me staring at him. Ugh.

First class was called and of course the two perfect specimens got up and strolled to the line. We wouldn't want them to have those looks and be poor.

I couldn't help but watch them as they headed down the tarmac. I felt a little bit like a stalker. They slipped out of sight, and I suddenly got antsy to get on the plane myself, just so I could stride by them again.

Get your crap together, I muttered to myself, causing an old lady in front of me to give me a sharp glance.

The airplane was almost full when they finally called my section, perks of buying the cheapest flight available...which honestly still wasn't that cheap since it was the holidays.

Someone bumped me from behind and I dropped my bag. The top of it ripped open, and I moaned when some books tumbled out. I was so flustered by the time I got on the plane, that I'd all but forgotten the two hotties from before.

That changed quickly when I began to walk through first class and saw them. The dark-haired one was already nursing a beer, and the blonde one held a tumbler in his hand full of some kind of amber colored drink, probably a fancy liquor.

It must be nice to have that kind of money, I thought to myself a little bitterly as my bag popped another stitch, threatening to spill its contents all over the aisle.

I tried to keep my eyes from gazing at them as I passed by, but of course I couldn't do that. They were both looking at me when I turned to gaze at them, and I was sure that my face turned a bright cherry red when our eyes met.

The dark-haired one winked at me again while the blonde just watched me stoically. I hurried past them, bumping the person in front of me who shot a glare over his shoulder. I was still blushing when I got to my seat. Of course, it was the middle seat in the very back row.

At least I won't have to go far for the bathrooms, I tried to reassure myself as I heard a toilet flush through the thin wall behind me.

I picked up my phone to check Facebook before the flight took off.

I had a message waiting for me from Todd, the creepiest stepbrother you could imagine. He was a year older than me, but there was some kind of screw loose in his head. Whenever I went home for breaks, he always managed to be there as well. I couldn't tell you the number of times my butt had been groped passing him in the hallway and I always made sure to lock my door while I slept just in case he decided to creep in while I was sleeping. I shivered and deleted his message without reading it. *No, thank you.*

My thoughts flickered to the guys currently sitting in first class. Why couldn't my stepbrother have looked like one of them? Not that I would ever have done anything with a hot stepbrother to begin with, but...

I was the quintessential good girl. I'd really never done a darn thing out of line in my life. See, I couldn't even say the word d-a-m-n. Probably the naughtiest thing I'd ever done was to pick a college in California when my dad had wanted me to stay close to home.

Not that he cared about that after step-monster came into the picture.

I leaned back into my seat and sighed.

I had one semester of college left after I got back from Christmas break, and what did I have to show for three and a half years of angelic behavior? Nothing. My grades weren't even all A's.

My phone buzzed again just as the flight attendant reminded us to turn off our phones in preparation for take off.

Can't wait to get close to you this break.

I gagged. It was Todd again. I didn't know what his deal was. Not responding once again, I turned off my phone and closed my eyes, trying not to lean too far left or too far right and bother my seatmates. The one to the left of me had a bad case of body odor. I opened my eyes once the smell got to be too much, and I leaned over to grab my bag, pulling out my favorite peppermint lotion. I knew it was bad etiquette to open something that smelled strong on an airplane, but I was fairly positive that everyone in these back rows would much rather smell "Holiday Peppermint" then my neighbor's smelly underarms.

The plane began to accelerate down the runway as I finished applying my lotion. Leaning back in my chair, I put on my head-phones, turned on Taylor Swift, and settled in for the flight.

I woke up suddenly when it felt like the plane was falling out of the sky. My stomach rose up to my throat, and I looked outside. We were flying through a white-out. Far different than the sunny skies we had left behind in California.

I had never liked flying, especially in turbulence like this. I let out a small squeak when the plane shuddered once again. The seatbelt sign flicked on and an announcement came on just then from the pilot.

"Sorry folks, looks like we will be experiencing some turbulence until we get to Chicago O'Hare. The storms a lot worse than antici-pated. Please stay in your seats and we'll let you know when it's safe to get up."

I began to grip my armrests for dear life as he finished. I loved how he had said "some" turbulence as the airplane once again felt like it was falling out of the sky. Another thirty minutes passed like this, and by the time the pilot announced that we were descending, my nerves were shot.

We landed, and I was so glad to be on the ground that I didn't even mind when my smelly neighbor let out a fart that sounded, and smelled, like it had come from an elephant.

When I stepped off the plane, I wanted to kiss the ground. Looking out the windows of the airport I could see that this was a really bad storm. My flight to New York was probably going to be just as bad with turbulence. I shivered just thinking about it.

I grabbed a Starbucks, my favorite white chocolate peppermint mocha of course, and set off for my gate. Chicago O'Hare was huge, and it took me ten minutes to get there. As I walked up to the gate I was dismayed to see that the flight had been delayed by two hours.

I walked over to the front desk to talk to the airline employee and get more details. There was a line of anxious people, all complaining about the delay to the stressed out employee.

I moved closer to hear what she was telling everyone.

"Sorry, ma'am. Until we are given the all clear, all aircrafts are grounded. We are hoping the storm passes soon and flights can recommence. It's going to be at least a few more hours though," the flustered employee told the woman standing in front of her who looked like she was about to cry.

The employee's eyes flickered over to me and she smiled softly, probably a practiced smile she offered all commuters stuck here.

I decided not to bother her since she wasn't going to say anything different to me. I stepped aside from the crowd of people that continued to line up to hear the same terrible news. Looking through the floor to ceiling windows that all airports seemed to have, I watched the snow blanket everything in sight. The planes. The runway. The buildings in the distance. The wind howled, blurring the view with white dust. I shivered just looking at the horrible weather.

The storm of the century had hit the day I landed in Chicago, leaving me and everyone else stuck due to our delayed flight. So what now? From the looks of it and the weather report I had pulled up on my phone, it didn't seem like it was going to be a delay of just a few hours.

Glancing down at my phone, I sent my best friend, Myles, a quick message.

Stuck in Chicago. Flight to NYC delayed due to storm. Hope it's just a few hours.

...

I waited for her response to pop up.

The weather is nasty here too, but I'm sure it will pass soon. In the meantime, find a hot guy. Tell him you're not wearing any underwear then walk away. He'll buy you drinks all night to pass the time.

My cheeks flushed just reading the words, and I looked around in case anyone had read her reply over my shoulder. Myles always sent the most insane messages. I quickly typed back a response.

Don't tell me you've actually done that?

Maybe. But girl, you'll never guess who I saw at the mall today. Your douche ex, Liam.

I furiously typed back, my blood boiling just reading his name. The dick had cheated on me, then tried to blame me, and dumped me via text.

Let me guess, I typed. *He got into another fight?*

He was with this girl, but don't worry, she wasn't that pretty and had greasy hair. They were kissing, so I bumped into them and told her he's a pig.

I laughed to myself as I typed, *You go girl.*

"Oh, look she's smiling," a guy said, flirtatiously, and I glanced up to see the infuriatingly cute dark-haired guy from the plane with those blue eyes I could easily lose myself in.

"I'm standing right here? I can hear you," I answered, feeling like I was back in high school.

His friend with the blonde hair and sharp cheekbones that looked like they belonged on a moviestar, nodded. "Pretty sure she's smiling because she's going to join us for a drink at the bar."

I rolled my eyes and snorted before turning back to my phone, although my cheeks were blushing from their attention. Myles hadn't responded yet but her suggestion on passing the time slid over my thoughts. I stiffened. Not in this lifetime. That wasn't who I was.

"What have you got to lose?" Blondie asked.

"Hmm let me see. My life if you two end up being serial killers."

Sexy Blue Eyes burst out laughing so hard that he teared up, drawing attention from the line-up of angry passengers. I mean, I couldn't deny that the sound of his laugh was the most delicious thing I'd ever heard. Loud, deep, and sexy as hell. Both of them were so hot it ought to be illegal.

"Thanks for that, Perky. I needed a good laugh." Blue Eyes' gaze dropped to my chest in a fleeting moment, and I resisted the urge to cross my arms.

"Excuse me?"

"Well, you haven't given us your name, and you seem to have a super "perky" personality," the Blonde replied, his green eyes staring at me with a secret hunger. His friend smirked, hands deep in the pockets of his jeans as he tried to recover from laughing so hard.

I narrowed my eyes at them, and I pushed aside the tingling in my gut that these two hot guys were actually talking to me. "You know you could ask me what my name is. How would you feel if I called you muscles and your friend... I don't know." I glanced around for a clue as my mind was foggy in their presence and having two against one had me flustered. My gaze swept over a poster of a salad. "Cucumber," I blurted and the moment the word left my mouth, I froze. What had I been thinking. *Stupid. Stupid. Stupid.*

"I'd say you were very accurate," Blondie answered in a droll voice, his amused gaze never leaving me. I could feel the heat shooting up my spine and over my neck and cheeks. I wasn't sure if the fire was my embarrassment at these two for teasing me or just me daydreaming because two gorgeous specimens were talking to me. I would go with the first one even though it was a lie. Good thing I could give back as good as I got.

"I'm not in the mood for douchebags today, thanks." I spun on my heel with my beat up handbag under my arm and dragged the wheely onboard luggage behind me.

My body burned up from the inside out, and I felt their eyes on my back. Somehow I ended up putting an extra swing in my hips before merging into the chaos of crowds...which was so unlike me.

Then I ran to the bathroom.

Who in the world did they think they were? Perky, please.

I stood in front of the full length mirror near the sinks. My nipples were at full mast, pressed against my white shirt, and I almost died. Shit! I rubbed them with my palm until they settled down. My cheeks burned the color of a cherry, my hair was sticking upward on one side, and I had a black smear on one knee of my jeans. Kill me now.

Taking a huge breath of air, I quickly collected a paper towel, dabbed it with water, and cleaned the dirt off as best I could. Digging in my handbag, I pulled out my comb, taming my golden hair that always bounced with a loose curl over my shoulders. With the lipstick, I colored my lips a shade of nude with a hint of pink. Just enough to stand out, but not too much to look slutty.

I grimaced that I'd just recited Gloria's words. Gloria was the step-monster and her insults and orders were always in my head even when I hadn't seen her for months.

I applied a few more layers of lipstick for a darker finish as a subtle "f.u." to the thought of her. There, now I looked fantastic.

Staring at myself in the mirror at my blue eyes, I couldn't help but think of my Mom. I hadn't taken after much of her looks with my curvy frame and average five-foot five height. She had been tall and thin, like a model.

But I had gotten her eyes. My dad had always told me after she passed that he saw her in my eyes every time he looked at me.

I leaned in closer to the mirror, swearing if I looked deep enough into my eyes, it felt like she was with me again. My breath misted the mirror. My heart clenched with sorrow because I missed her terribly, especially at Christmas. When she'd make her famous Portugese turkey roast, decorate the whole house with way too many Santa Claus's, and insist we sang carols. I used to hate doing them, now... now I'd give anything in the world to hear her persistent voice, her excited voice, her loving voice.

I swallowed the lump in my throat when someone moved behind me. I quickly stepped back from the mirror, wiped away the loose tear, and tossed everything in my handbag. In haste, I made my way to the toilet.

Back in the main area of the airport, I strolled with my wheelie bag behind me, past crowds of people, looking into the big branded stores I could never afford. Each cafe I walked past was jam packed with a line out the door. When I found no line in front of the sports bar, I marched inside to the bar, noticing people were everywhere. Large screens dotted the walls, playing all the latest sports, and the air smelled of beer and fried food. Perfect.

"What will you have?" a woman's voice asked, and I turned to find the bartender offering me a curt smile, clear she'd been run off her feet from the influx of stranded passengers.

"Too early in the day for a Margarita?"

She half chuckled. "Ma'am, in my books, it's never too early."

I rarely drank, but right now I felt like drowning myself in something delicious.

"Sounds perfect. Can I get the nachos too, please?"

"Absolutely. Take a seat, and I'll bring everything out to you."

"Thanks." I turned to find a table, even sharing with someone would be perfect, as long as I just got to sit in peace and work out my next steps. Except, every single chair was filled, even along the window with the single seats.

Someone waved to me from across the room at a tall table with three seats around it. Two of the seats were taken. The moment my eyes laid on those two arrogant jerks, my stomach dropped.

A smile crossed Blue Eyes' lips, and I shook my head, then walked towards the far window, figuring I was bound to find something. All I needed was one chair and I'd squeeze in another table. But it wasn't long before I realized that luck wasn't on my side, and I glimpsed over my shoulder at them. Both were staring at me, probably laughing, and I sighed.

"Hi, ma'am, where will you be sitting?"

I looked over to the lady from behind the bar holding my margarita in a hurricane glass and a large plate of nachos.

Panic crawled through me as I looked around the room.

"Over here," Blue Eyes called from his table. "She's sitting with us."

"Okay then." The waitress marched toward them.

I eyed them with my best glare, but Blondie just winked.

They were going to make me suffer. I knew it.

Deep breath.

Continue reading: https://books2read.com/u/3JVrle

ABOUT C.R. JANE

A Texas girl living in Utah now, I'm a wife, mother, lawyer, and now author. My stories have been floating around in my head for years, and it has been a relief to finally get them down on paper. I'm a huge Dallas Cowboys fan and I primarily listen to Beyonce and Taylor Swift...don't lie and say you don't too.

My love of reading started probably when I was three and with a faster than normal ability to read, I've devoured hundreds of thousands of books in my life. It only made sense that I would start to create my own worlds since I was always getting lost in others'. I like heroines who have to grow in order to become badasses, happy endings, and swoon-worthy, devoted, (and hot) male characters. If this sounds like you, I'm pretty sure we'll be friends. I'm so glad to have you on my team...check out the links below for ways to hang out with me and more of my books you can read!

Visit my **Facebook** page to get updates.

Visit my **Amazon Author** page.

Visit my **Website**.

Sign up for my **newsletter** to stay updated on new releases, find out random facts about me, and get access to different points of view from my characters.

OTHER BOOKS BY C.R. JANE

The Fated Wings Series

First Impressions

Forgotten Specters

The Fallen One (a Fated Wings Novella)

Forbidden Queens

Frightful Beginnings (a Fated Wings Short Story)

Faded Realms

Faithless Dreams

The Rock God (a Fated Wings Novella)

The Timeless Affection Series

Lamented Pasts

Lost Passions

The Pack Queen Series

Queen of the Thieves

Queen of the Alphas (2019)

The Rise Again Series

The Day After Nothing (2020)

The Sounds of Us Contemporary Series

Remember Us This Way

Remember You This Way

Remember Me This Way

Broken Hearts Academy Series

Heartbreak Prince

Academy of Souls Co-write with Mila Young

School of Broken Souls

School of Broken Hearts

School of Broken Dreams

Fallen World Series Co-write with Mila Young

Bound

Broken

Betrayed

Standalone Co-write with Mila Young

The Naughty List

Stupid Boys Series Co-write with Rebecca Royce

Stupid Boys

Dumb Girl

ABOUT MILA YOUNG

Mila Young tackles everything with the zeal and bravado of the fairy-tale heroes she grew up reading about. She slays monsters, real and imaginary, like there's no tomorrow. By day she rocks a keyboard as a marketing extraordinaire. At night she battles with her might pen-sword, creating fairytale retellings, and sexy ever after tales. In her spare time, she loves pretending she's a mighty warrior, walks on the beach with her dogs, cuddling up with her cats, and devouring every fantasy tale she can get her pinkies on.

Join my **Facebook** reader group.

Visit my **Amazon Author** page.

Sign up for my **newsletter** for newest releases, exclusive excerpts, giveaways and loads of games.

OTHER BOOKS BY MILA YOUNG

Gods and Monsters

Apollo Is Mine

Poseidon Is Mine

Ares Is Mine

Hades Is Mine

Winter's Thorn

To Seduce A Fae

Haven Realm Series

Hunted (Little Red Riding Hood Retelling)

Cursed (Beauty and the Beast Retelling)

Entangled (Rapunzel Retelling)

Wicked Heat Series

Wicked Heat #1

Wicked Heat #2

Wicked Heat #3

Elemental Series

Taking Breath #1

Taking Breath #2

Fallen World Series Co-write with C.R. Jane

Bound

Broken

Betrayed

Broken Souls Series Co-write with C.R. Jane

School of Broken Souls

School of Broken Hearts

School of Broken Dreams

Beautiful Beasts Academy Co-write with Kim Faulks

Manicures and Mayhem

Diamonds and Demons

Hexes and Hounds

Secrets and Shadows

Passions and Protectors

Ancients and Anarchy

Printed in the USA
CPSIA information can be obtained
at www.ICGtesting.com
LVHW042139121123
763741LV00035B/234